ALSO BY POLLY HORVATH

the Night Garden

POLLY HORVATH

FARRAR STRAUS GIROUX
NEW YORK

Farrar Straus Giroux Books for Young Readers
An imprint of Macmillan Publishing Group, LLC
175 Fifth Avenue, New York, NY 10010

Printed in the United States of America by LSC Communications, Harrisonburg, Virginia
First edition, 2017
10 9 8 7 6 5 4 3 2 1

mackids.com

Library of Congress Cataloging-in-Publication Data

Names: Horvath, Polly, author.
Title: The night garden / Polly Horvath.
Description: First edition. | New York : Farrar Straus Giroux, 2017. | Summary:
    Twelve-year-old Franny Whitekraft lives quietly with her adopted parents on
    a farm on Vancouver Island until the spring of 1945, when the three Madden children
    move in, UFOs and ghosts appear, an important military airplane disappears, and
    wishes made in Old Tom's forbidden night garden will hopefully get everyone
    out of trouble. |
Identifiers: LCCN 2016043678 (print) | LCCN 2017022544 (ebook) | ISBN
    9780374304546 (ebook) | ISBN 9780374304522 (hardcover)
Subjects: | CYAC: Wishes—Fiction. | Adoption—Fiction. | World War,
    1939–1945—Fiction. | British Columbia—Fiction. | Canada—Fiction.
Classification: LCC PZ7.H79224 (ebook) | LCC PZ7.H79224 Ni 2017 (print) |
    DDC [Fic]—dc23
LC record available at https://lccn.loc.gov/2016043678

Our books may be purchased in bulk for promotional, educational, or business use. Please
contact your local bookseller or the Macmillan Corporate and Premium Sales Department
at (800) 221-7945 ext. 5442 or by e-mail at MacmillanSpecialMarkets@macmillan.com.

To Arnie, Emily and John,
Rebecca, Andrew and Zayda

ONTENTS

A Little Background

This is the story of Winifred, Wilfred, and Zebediah; Crying Alice; and Flying Bob. It is in part the story of Thomasina and Old Tom. It is only in small part my story, but I get to do the telling. My name is Franny, and I am living with Thomasina and Old Tom because of a series of mistakes involving their neighbors. Old Tom always calls Thomasina Thomasina. But I have always addressed her as Sina because when I was little "Thomasina" was too difficult for me to say. When I was just a baby I was supposed to be adopted by the family who lived next door to Sina and Old Tom, but the night before this was to happen the neighbors' house burned down and the neighbors burned with it. No one bothered to inform the adoption agency. The caseworker knocked on Sina and Old Tom's door, and when Sina answered the caseworker said, "I was supposed to drop this baby off next door, but there appears to be no next door."

Sina stuck her head around the door and spied the smoke. The smoldering embered remains of our neighbors' house were quite a ways down the lonely stretch of coastal farm road, but across our eastern cove you could see what was left of the house. It was the smoke billowing above the waters that Sina was staring at when she said, "So there doesn't."

Old Tom came into the front hall and said, "Ah, that's what all the commotion was about last night."

"Can you hold the baby?" asked the caseworker, handing me to Old Tom. "I seem to be having a pain."

Old Tom passed me to Sina. "I don't have much to do with babies if I can help it," he said. "It's not that I don't like them. I just don't know what to do with them."

Then while Sina held me and she and Old Tom looked on, the caseworker had a heart attack and died right there on the doorstep.

"My goodness," said Sina.

"I guess we'll have to keep her," said Old Tom, meaning me, not the caseworker. He knelt down to see if she required anything in the way of CPR. She was quite dead, but he tried anyway. "You have to," he told me whenever he related the oft-told tale. "Even though it is clear it will do no good. You have to try anyway if you belong to the Church of Lost Causes."

There is no such church. It was just something that Old Tom said a lot. Perhaps he had a whole liturgy of lost causes going on in his head. Perhaps he peopled it with a whole hierarchy of clergy. Who knows? Or perhaps it was just something he said to amuse himself. A little wry comment on his character.

"We shall call her Franny," said Sina.

"Francesca," said Old Tom, nodding. "It's a noble name."

"No," said Sina. "Franny. Not short for anything. I can tell she's going to be a serious, practical, and realistic person. I can feel it in my bones."

Old Tom never argued with Sina's bones.

"I don't suppose there's anything left of the baby stuff next door," said Sina, pondering the smoking ruins.

After that Old Tom called an ambulance to take away the dead body. When the ambulance workers had done so, Old Tom and Sina, carrying me, walked over to look at the smoking ruins from enough angles to determine that there would indeed be no salvageable baby stuff.

As far as the adoption agency was concerned, the goods had been delivered. As far as the ambulance personnel were concerned, the body of the caseworker was now their problem. As far as Sina and Old Tom were concerned, any adoption agency so inept that they couldn't keep track of their deliveries had had their chance with me. Now the fates had put me with them, and I was their problem.

"Tom, go into Victoria and buy diapers and baby furniture and bottles and formula and anything else that occurs to you. I will take Franny and show her the house."

Sina showed me the first floor, with the parlor, the library, the kitchen, the dining and living rooms with their big fireplaces, the sun room, and the attached greenhouse, which is really Old Tom's domain even though it is in the house, which is Sina's domain. Then up to the second floor, with the four bedrooms. Two of those face the south and the sea. They belong to Sina and Old Tom.

Although they are married, you would be forgiven for thinking they were distant cousins or something because they are both in their own little worlds most of the time and Old Tom is a foot shorter than Sina, which seems strange in a husband/wife situation somehow. I mean, you can't choose the height of other people. But you'd think people sizing up prospective spouses would, in the back of their minds, be looking for someone nearer their own height if only to make kissing more convenient. Or, at most, having the man taller by a foot than the woman. I believe it's really very unusual the other way around. But Sina is rather tall for a woman and Old Tom is a bit on the short side for a man, although neither is freakishly so. In addition, Sina is all caught up in her sculpting and Old Tom in his gardens, and when they sit across from each other at the little kitchen table, both just having happened to find themselves there in the late afternoon for a cup of tea, they often hardly seem to notice each other. I have come across them contemplatively eating biscuits and staring moodily out the window to the sea, and if I say hello they turn to me and answer, "Hello, Franny," and then seem to suddenly notice each other and jump. I'm used to it but other people might find it odd, is all I'm saying.

Anyway, I have a bedroom facing the back with one window from which I can just see the ocean where it curves around toward Beechey Head. I get the sunsets from there. And then there's an empty bedroom, and up one floor from there are six small maid's rooms (but no maids) and an attic storage room. It's quite the Victorian wedding cake of a house.

There's the bathroom with the clawfoot tub on the second floor. And the bathroom with the regular tub on the third floor. But no toilets. Because the house is Victorian, running water is a recent addition, but Old Tom and Sina never put in toilets or electricity. I asked Old Tom about this once and he said by the time they were done with the commotion of putting in the running water and workmen, workmen, workmen everywhere, they hadn't the heart for it. I can quite understand. We have always led a wonderfully peaceful life, never bothered by family, friends, or visitors. So the intrusion of the running-water people must have been dreadful, but it was all done before I joined them. Sina said thank goodness it was, too, because after I got there, diapers became, for a time, the story of her life.

Finally, on top, there is the cupola, which has wide windows on all four sides and which just sat there unused until I claimed it. Out back, Sina has a sculpture studio where she works all day. Old Tom works in his gardens and on the farm. And, of course, there is the daily care of the animals with which we all help. Twenty leghorn chickens, two plow horses, five jersey cows, and a bull. Pigs coming and pigs going, which means don't get too attached to the pigs. Pigs are very smart. Smarter than dogs, some people say, and let's face it, you don't want anything of great intelligence looking up at you from your dinner plate. It doesn't seem to bother Old Tom too terribly, but then you'd never know. He isn't one to suffer visibly.

From every room in the house except the extra bedroom and four of the maid's rooms and the parlor, you can see the ocean. The property is in Sooke on the coast of Vancouver Island in British Columbia, and called East Sooke Farm. We are close to British Columbia's capital, Victoria, and so Victoria is the city we use when we need one, which isn't often.

From my cupola, with my telescope, I can see whales—orcas and humpbacks and occasionally a gray whale that has gone missing from its friends while making its migration down the west coast of North America, mistakenly taking a detour and floundering up the Juan de Fuca Strait. Quite often all you see is it spouting. Gray whales can stay under for a long time. I also see otters, seals, sea lions, cougars, bears, eagles, hawks, rabbits, voles, squirrels, and sometimes unidentifiable things. You used to see wolves. Now not so much.

Old Tom said they once had a hired girl helping with the pigs and the milking, and one day she came into the house exclaiming about the nice "set of dogs" that had suddenly shown up, all friendly-like and accompanying her to the creamery. When Old Tom told her what they really were she fainted dead away. Which is silly, I said to Old Tom. I mean, they weren't any different at that moment than they'd been when she'd been hanging out with them. It does go to show that so much of your experience is based not on fact but on what you choose to believe about things. Her experience was of nice, friendly animals, but she couldn't make that jibe with what she knew about Little Red Riding Hood. Even though you don't see a lot of wolves anymore, sometimes you hear them. At least Old Tom and I do. Sina says they are dogs, but she is not always right—although like me, and I guess Old Tom, too, and, come to think of it, everyone, she always thinks she is.

While Sina showed me the house, Old Tom left to get me what I needed. He wasn't sure what all that was, but he stopped any maternal-looking woman he could find on Douglas Street in Victoria and between all of them they cobbled together the necessary supplies. One bossy woman dragged him into Eaton's, Victoria's only department store, and told him what else he had to have. She even picked out the crib and would let him have no say. Old Tom says there's always one bossy woman around. But he didn't mind because he just wanted to get it over with and get back to his gardening.

Then Old Tom came home and, while Sina set things up in the nursery, he showed me his gardens, scattered beyond and around the hayfields. I was perhaps a mite young to appreciate it all, but I'm sure I was lulled by his voice. Old Tom has a gravelly voice, but it is oddly soothing because of this. It is a voice worn into chunkiness and rough edges by time. It is as soothing as an old quilt or the ocean boulders you can sit on because they are smoothed every day and night by the tides. He showed me the English garden and the herb garden. He showed me the Italian garden and the statuary garden. He showed me the kitchen garden and the apple orchard. He showed me the wildflower garden and the garden of exotic blooms and the Japanese garden and the heliotrope garden. But he did not show me the night garden. That one Old Tom kept locked up.

Then he walked me down the rocky path to show me all the little coves and beaches. Old Tom had a boat he took out to fish if the ocean wasn't too choppy. It was anchored on a short dock on the quiet side of one of the coves. Then, coming up the steep old stairs from the beach to the field that leads to the house, he almost dropped me. That's when it occurred to him that they had taken on a whole new human being, and the weight of the responsibility, he said, was pressing. He said this to Sina as he came in the back door.

"But we must take on what comes at us in life, or we are worthless worms," said Sina.

Sina had decided opinions and liked things black-and-white. Old Tom was more apt to see the advantages of letting matters be gray. But I swear I remember this, coming up from the ocean, being held so that my eyes beheld the naked light of the sky and the eagles swooping and the flight of one lone heron. I was filled with a happiness so large that it seemed to have no boundaries from around me to it to the sky to this stretch of land and sea and field. I am home, I thought happily, I am as home as anyone in this earthly life can be. And Sina and Old Tom often wondered that I didn't cry more or carry on, but who could be happier than to be growing in all that light and changing sky and life, and I was part of it.

I had dinner that very first night on their dining room table, propped up in the baby seat that Tom had bought, and I slept peacefully every night after. Sina said that the first few months of my life at their house she found herself talking to the walls quite a bit because she felt she needed to relate to someone the momentousness of what was going on, and Old Tom was always in the garden. And every night after dinner she settled down in the rocking chair on the second-floor landing, which has a floor-to-ceiling window overlooking the sea. She rocked and rocked and gazed and gazed at the horizon, where the sea stopped and the sky began. She said she had often rocked there but it was different with a baby. It had a more grounded, more anchored weight to it and at the same time a kind of link to a great, nebulous future.

The first night as she rocked, Old Tom went out to the kitchen garden as he often did after dinner.

"You don't mind, do you? Taking on a baby?" she called to him from the window.

"Would it matter if I did?" he called back over his shoulder.

"Probably not," she said to herself. "At any rate, for all of us, Franny, for you and me and Old Tom, everything is now changed. But that is the whole of what life is. See the sun sinking over the edge of the sea? This day is done. This day will never come again. Everything has changed. Remind yourself of that every morning and every night, and then you won't come to expect anything but what is. It's expecting anything but what is that makes people unhappy."

I don't know if I heard her that first night, but as she gave that speech a fair bit at sundown, I heard it enough times afterward to have it memorized.

And then I grew up. At least to twelve, which seems plenty grown to me, and this was when Crying Alice made her entrance and, of course, that changed everything, too.

CRYING ALICE

**W**hen it all began I was upstairs in my cupola working on my history of the farm. Tomorrow was the last day of school for a while because its roof was about to collapse. Finding a steady crew to fix it had been difficult. It was 1945 and the whole world seemed to be at war and practically all our able men who usually did these sorts of things had been shipped overseas, so the roof repair was going to take twice as long as it would have in times of peace. It was just one more reason to hate the Nazis, said our principal.

There was nowhere else to put us during the reconstruction, so it was decided that we would have our summer vacation in the spring and go to school in the summer after the roof was fixed. They tried to be upbeat by calling it a special spring vacation, but it fooled no one. We were to be done out of our summer, and this was very hard on the families who needed their children to help bring in the hay. But it meant I would have whole weeks to really dig into my writing. I got a lot of writing done during school holidays, especially the summer one. But not a lot during the school year, as our school was quite a long way from the farm. To get there, I left early in the morning. I had to walk across our fields to Becher Bay Road and all the way down that to East Sooke Road, where I would catch the school bus for the long trip to school. Then there was time *in* school, which I always enjoyed, after which the long trip in reverse to get home and by the time I got there, I usually didn't have the requisite creative energy to work.

Old Tom, when he found out I was a writer, bought me a magnificent rolltop desk in a junk store in Victoria. He had it delivered and put into the cupola to surprise me. It had secret drawers. Then he found me a typewriter, and he was very good about keeping me supplied with paper. I always think of Sina as the giver of presents and such, but the best presents I have ever gotten have been from Old Tom because, although he doesn't do it often and he doesn't say much when he does, he somehow knows exactly who I am and what I want. Once I commented on the poster in our doctor's office called "The Land of Make Believe." I was besotted. It was full of fairy-tale figures on a mysterious dark black background—everywhere you looked was magic and enchantment—and two weeks later, quietly swollen with suppressed pride, Old Tom brought home a framed copy and hung it in my bedroom.

Sometimes I stared at it for inspiration. But at night after school and dinner, when I was tired and sitting at my desk, I just stared into the darkness outside. You could see an amazing array of stars from my cupola.

I had thought about hauling out the mermaid story I was currently working on but which wasn't going well. It had reached the point all my stories did, where I simply put them in the lowest desk drawer and abandoned them. When this happened I worked on a history of the farm, nonfiction being easier than fiction because you had something concrete to start from. With fiction you were starting with nothing. No, not with nothing—with something that you had to bring into readable being from some amorphous state you could only sense.

The farm itself seemed to have elements as mysterious as the poster Old Tom gave to me. It was hard to know why. Why does one piece of land seem to be alive and breathing with suppressed something—potential,

becoming, intelligent energy? There were the petroglyphs on our rocky coast pointing to people living here
thousands of years ago. There were the generations of
people who had owned the place such as Mrs. Brown,
who had five children and had to sell off large tracts of
land bit by bit to various buyers to pay her taxes in order
to keep a small piece of land and the house. The house
that now belonged to Old Tom, Sina, and me. The man
who bought the majority of the tracts eventually convinced Mrs. Brown to sell the little she'd kept back and,
sadly, finally even the house and then turned it from
her farm into a summer place. He built tennis courts,
now long gone, plowed up and made into a potato field
by my great-aunt Bertha, who bought his property and
the tracts Mrs. Brown had sold to others so that the 270
acres were one again. Aunt Bertha left it all to Old Tom
when she died. She told Old Tom the tennis-court
people had fabulous parties with Japanese lanterns and
women in white gowns and important personages—all
that glamour gone, and yet it still seemed to linger in
the air with everything else: the people who had lived
here thousands of years ago; the sadness of Mrs. Brown;
the ridiculousness of Aunt Bertha, who, according to Old
Tom, was as wide as she was tall and given to outbursts.

He said she reminded him of a short, squat caboose chugging around the farm with steam coming from her ears. I don't know if the land became what it is from the people who lived on it or the people became what they did from absorbing something from the land. I found all the history interesting and got it whenever I could in bits and pieces by asking all the old-timers in Sooke, everyone I met really, for their memories. But no one remembered much. And as interesting as those snippets were, none of it accounted for what I felt on the place, what the land seemed to be communicating.

So I didn't mind working on the history if no fiction came to me. I thought it was important to keep doing some kind of writing. It always made me feel better. As if there were some kind of special energy available but outside of me that I could pull in and it would move through me, coming out my fingers onto the blank page as neither entirely itself nor me but something new. Nothing on the page ever quite lived up to the glimpse of the glimmer of that magic. It was the hope that someday it would that kept me going back to it.

On this particular night, I was drumming my fingers aimlessly on my typewriter wishing I had more personal anecdotes about Mrs. Brown and her children and wondering if I couldn't just make some up, when I heard a commotion below, but the cupola is so far from the first floor that I couldn't make out any words. I tried to see whose car was in the driveway, but it was too dark.

After the back door slammed and the person left, I peered out again and realized they must have walked over because there was no sound of a car starting up and I could see a flashlight beam head off across the fields. I knew it had to be one of our far-flung neighbors. When the person got to Becher Bay Road and it was clear that they were truly gone for the night, and that I wouldn't have to speak to them, I went downstairs and Sina told me what had happened.

Mrs. Madden, otherwise known as Crying Alice, had charged over to our house.

"Yoohoo, Mrs. Whitekraft!" Sina heard her call as she opened the front door and came into the front hall uninvited. "Mrs. Whitekraft? I know we haven't gotten to know each other greatly. Or even very well. Or even at all. But now I need you. I NEED you, Mrs. Whitekraft. Thomasina?" And Alice began to bawl. Crying was what Alice did best.

Sina and I had named her Crying Alice after we had compared notes about all the places we had seen her cry.

We had seen her cry at parent-teacher conferences for no apparent reason. I didn't know much about her children because they were all in different grades from me, but they appeared to be very good citizens, good students, upstanding humans, as Old Tom would say. Nothing to cry over.

We had seen her cry when there were no eggs left at Brookman's. Brookman's was on the edge of Sooke and the closest store for all the far-flung residents, and so the hub of a lot of its social life. On Saturdays we brought our eggs and milk to sell there, and the ladies met there to chat in the morning.

We had seen Alice cry at school Christmas concerts.

"Well, really," said Sina, clearing her throat in embarrassment when we got to this part. "That could happen to anyone."

Sina had a soft spot for gently lisping carolers.

Alice didn't just cry a lot; she cried in situations where normal people seem to be able to hold it together. She cried when she got mud on her dress. She cried when her car got a flat. She cried when she saw the new kittens at Brookman's. She cried when dropping her children off for their first day of school in the fall. And once Old Tom and I had caught her crying while her car was being filled up with gas. We just sat there in our truck watching in fascination until she pulled away.

"That is one unhappy dame," said Old Tom.

When Sina told the ladies at Brookman's that we had named Alice Madden "Crying Alice," they approved. Then they told us her husband did maintenance for the Canadian Air Force's special plane, the *Argot*, in Comox and called himself Fixing Bob, which made the nickname Crying Alice seem coincidentally but pleasingly mated. I thought perhaps all couples should have similarly paired nicknames. I tried out Old Tom and Tall Sina, both being one-syllable adjectives, but it didn't work at all.

Anyhow, when Crying Alice entered the house wailing, Sina had been drafting her thirty-seventh letter to William Lyon Mackenzie King, the prime minister of Canada, begging him for the sake of the country to grow a mustache like his predecessor, Robert Borden. *He was such a dish,* she wrote. *And you have such a baby face. I feel we would be taken more seriously on the international circuit . . .* Was this the expression she wanted? Were there circuits in international politics? Oh well, let *him* figure it out. He should be able to—he was the prime minister, after all.

It seems to me that the public figures people most pay attention to all have mustaches. Look at Hitler. Look at Mussolini. Look at Franco. Mustaches all. I'm not saying you want to be like these men. I'm just saying it's time that Canada got it together and distinguished itself, internationally speaking, and I fear we shall never be able to do it with a baby-faced prime minister. You were not my choice for prime minister. Your party (if I may be so bold as to tender an opinion) is all wet. But, nevertheless, now you are my prime minister and we must all just make the best of it. You obviously don't think grooming matters, so I am here to tell you it does and to lend you a little practical advice. I hope you will take it in the spirit in which it is meant.

Yours sincerely,

Thomasina Whitekraft

P.S. I'm sure even the voters who voted for your party—of which, as I say, I am not one—probably wish you'd do something to appear a little less doughy.

She was mumbling this last sentence to herself as she went down the hall to answer the wail. The sentence didn't sound quite right, so she was saying it out loud to herself, editing it. *Even the voters who voted for your party?* No, no, no, that's repetitive. *Even the citizens who voted for you?* Why say "citizens"? *I did not vote for you but if I had...?* No, that's all wrong. We don't vote directly for our prime minister. And "doughy" is perhaps a little harsh. Accurate but harsh.

She was so preoccupied by this that she had forgotten why she'd walked to the front door and didn't even notice Crying Alice standing in the front hall dripping tears all over the floor. Sina walked right around her to shut the door.

"Good lord, does no one pay attention to drafts?" she asked, heading back to the kitchen where her typewriter was set up.

"Mrs. Whitekraft!" said Crying Alice.

Sina heard this, whipped her head around, and jumped about four feet in the air. At this point Alice was crying so hard that she was leaning her face against the wall making hard-to-get-out wet marks, and all Sina saw was the back of a mass of unruly hair and because her mind was on other things, her first thought was that a large soggy dog had somehow gotten into the house and was dripping on her wall. But, of course, after that she quickly changed gears, came partly down to earth, and realized it was a person. It was the clothes, she explained to me later.

"Oh my God, are you a burglar?" she asked. Then she noticed that some of the wetness on the walls was from the burglar's heaving, sobbing body. "Are you a burglar already repenting? Get out. Get out and I shan't report you to the police."

"Mrs. Whitekraft, I am not a burglar," said Crying Alice. "Didn't you hear me before? Don't you recognize me? I'm your neighbor."

Well, of course, Sina came fully down to earth then, realized exactly what she had on her hands, and was not happy about it.

"What are you doing breaking into homes? Do you call that neighborly? Get out." Sina wanted to get back to her letter. She was losing her train of thought. It didn't occur to her that there was any kind of situation at hand just because Alice was crying. Alice was *always* crying.

"I have a very great favor to ask you," said Crying Alice, sobbing.

"The answer is no," said Sina. "We can't have people just charging into our homes and upsetting the order of things. I'm trying to write a letter and you've put me completely off."

"You must help me. You must," cried Alice.

"Why must I?" asked Sina.

"Because I'm afraid my husband is going to do something stupid."

"What kind of stupid?"

"Dangerously stupid. I feel it in my bones," said Crying Alice, blowing her nose.

"Oh, all right," snapped Sina, who always paid attention to the things she felt in her own bones. "It will put a crimp in my evening, I can see that already, but come into the kitchen and tell me all about it."

SINA TELLS ME

hen Sina had finished relating all of this, I said, "My goodness, what was the great favor?"

"I've agreed to take the children of Crying Alice Madden," said Sina.

"Surely not," I said, grabbing two Girl Guide cookies out of the jar. This struck me as a two-cookie conundrum.

"Yes," said Sina. "And I've no idea why. Any number of people could have taken them. Why me?"

"Perhaps you secretly like small children," I suggested, sitting across from her and beginning on cookie number one.

"It would have to be very secretly," said Sina.

"Then perhaps it has become a sort of nervous tic

with you," I said, breaking the cookie into judicious bites to fuel my ideas. Bit of cookie, bit of idea, bit of cookie was the plan. "After all, you took me on."

"That was twelve years ago. Besides, you were different," said Sina. "I could see that right away. You were extraordinary. There was never going to be another you. Don't ask me to break into song. I shan't."

"Thank you," I said. "Not about the song part. Although thank you for that, too. About the extraordinary part."

"Not at all," said Sina. "Anyway, it's done now and it can't be undone. I've said that after school tomorrow she can drop off Winifred, Wilfred, and Zebediah and they can stay with us while she goes up to Comox."

"Oh," I said. This was a blow, but one must keep a stiff upper lip. "I see. Good thing we have all those maid's rooms they can stay in way up on the third floor where maybe we can pretend they aren't here."

This was rather tricky of me, implying as it did that these strange children would *of course* be living on the third floor and not on the second with the civilized folk.

"Yes. Good thing!" said Sina, seizing on this immediately. "Although it is rather a long way to the outhouse from there. Three flights of stairs."

"The back stairs are not so bad," I said. "A bit steep,

but they are swift if one's calls to nature are very pressing. We could keep a series of coal lanterns burning at strategic points."

"They'd trip on them and burn the house down. We had better move one of the rockers off the second floor landing, too. Boys can probably run around one rocker without breaking their necks, but two may issue too much of a challenge. Boys clatter. And we'll hand out flashlights."

"Yes, that should work splendidly. See, no problem at all," I said happily now that it was clear that the Madden children would be a whole floor away from me and, I decided, not allowed in the cupola under any circumstances. "Well, then, for how long?"

"That's just it. I really don't know. Because it was Alice, you see."

"Ah. So rather less talking, more crying?"

"Exactly," said Sina. "A *lot* of crying and general carrying-on. She seemed to think that unless she joined her husband immediately up at the air force base in Comox he was going to do something stupid."

"What kind of stupid?" I asked.

"Who knows? What kind of stupid things would a plane maintenance person do?"

"Drink the cleaning fluid?" I suggested. Sina and I loved this kind of speculation.

"Braid the mops?" suggested Sina.

"Perhaps it has nothing to do with his job," I said. "Perhaps she is afraid he is taking up the tarantella and if left unfettered would soon be moving the whole family to Italy."

"Italy?"

"It's where it originated. It's supposed to be mimicking what happens when you get bitten by a tarantula."

"Really, Franny, I don't know how you know these things," said Sina.

"I read."

"Anyhow, I suspect she knew more than she would let on. She seemed to feel her presence in Comox was urgent."

"That sounds bad," I said. "Bad or melodramatic. We really don't know her well enough to make a judgment call, do we?"

"No, that's what I thought. I asked if she thought he was going overseas to fight that evil Hitler, but she said no."

"Didn't she even give you a hint as to what she thought he might be up to?"

"No, she refused to say."

"The nerve," I said.

"Just so," said Sina. "You've hit the nail on the head; to come over and ask such a very great favor and make wet marks on my nice clean walls and yet refuse to give any juicy details—well, it defies all manners and sense."

We both looked out the window and I decided I was out of good ideas for the moment, so I finished the cookies in a couple of bites.

"Still, that's what we're stuck with. I think I'll go to bed," said Sina.

"Good idea," I said. And then something occurred to me. "Tomorrow is the last day of school before the special spring vacation. You don't suppose she means to leave them here all spring long?"

"I've no idea. Nobody tells me anything," said Sina despairingly, and she went up the stairs muttering, "Doughy or pasty-faced? Which is less apt to offend?"

I made my last trip to the outhouse before turning in and sat among the bats and insects thinking that having these strange children cluttering up our 270 acres this spring was not what any of us had planned and how everything can change in a blink.

Then I walked back toward the house. I could hear

the owls overhead, always there, always unseen, like tree monks chanting *who who who*, their mysterious plain-song, their mystical calls sent into the night, into the black unknown, calling to what we were all calling to, *who who who*, *where where where*, setting the universe right, steadying my tangents, piping me to bed.

They Arrive

ell, we are all put on this earth to suffer, and the next day after I'd gotten home from school Crying Alice drove Winifred, eleven; Wilfred, nine; and Zebediah, six, over to the house. Winifred and Wilfred looked similar. They both had long rangy limbs, sandy hair, and freckles. Wilfred, although younger, was taller than Winifred and wore horn-rimmed glasses that made his eyes large and owly. He had a front flop of hair that he was always brushing out of them. Winifred kept her long hair neat. Zebediah was short and dark with olive skin and black curly hair and could have come from a whole other family, so different was he from Winifred and Wilfred. They each carried a small duffel bag. I eyed the bags, trying to determine from the size of them exactly how long they would be staying. But it was difficult. They were medium bags. That could mean that Crying Alice was an over-packer and they would be with us for the weekend only (oh, please God), or she could be a severe under-packer, planning to park them with us for a few months, necessitating Sina taking them shopping. Or the children could lead a spartan existence, eschewing all but the bare necessities. In which case they would not be so appalled by the outhouse. I had had the odd girl over to play and they all seemed to think that by the time 1945 rolled around, everyone in the world should be in possession of an indoor flush toilet. As I had grown up with the outhouse, I had never considered us "strangely medieval," as one potential friend put it.

There we all stood in the front hallway eyeing each other.

Sina, I noticed, had the identical great false grin plastered on her face as I.

"There now," said Crying Alice. "Winifred, stand up straight. Wilfred, look alive. Zebediah, don't slouch. All right, children. I'm off to berate your father. I must talk Fixing Bob out of whatever it is he thinks he is going to do. Be good. Please try to eat healthily. I shall return as soon as I possibly can. Mrs. Whitekraft, may I say that this is contiguous of you."

"Contiguous?" said Sina. "Well, you certainly can *say* it . . ."

"Now, children, let us try to part cheerfully." At which point Crying Alice broke into hysterical sobs, turned on her heels, and barely made it to her car without flooding the front yard. We could see her bent over the wheel, driving off, her shoulders racked with heaving, shuddering sorrow but her hand waving cheerfully good-bye out the window until the car was no longer in sight.

I had to admire the children, because they looked more or less normal and unfazed by these theatrics and, really, with the example she set for them, we'd no right to expect it.

"Well, then," said Sina. "That's done. Dinner at six-thirty." She turned toward the kitchen, leaving me, as agreed, to show them around.

The children were delighted with their tiny third-floor rooms. The four of us stood in Winifred's.

"They're like little dollhouse rooms," said Winifred. "I got a room of my own for the first time when we moved here from the air force base in Comox. We used to live on base on Prince Edward Island before the air force moved the *Argot*, the very important plane that Daddy maintains, to the Comox base."

"Yes, I know," I said, not bothering to tell her how fast information moves in a small community. "Thus Fixing Bob."

"Yes, thus Fixing Bob. But Mother said she was tired of living on bases. We'd lived on three so far. And the houses are always teeny-tiny with not enough bedrooms, and the yards are teeny-tiny, and some people object to Mother crying so much."

"I suppose some might call her Crying Alice," I said tentatively. "Like Fixing Bob."

"Oh, how clever you are," said Winifred. "To think of that right on the spot."

"Well," I said, looking down modestly but not arguing, figuring we might as well establish this at the start.

"*Flying* Bob," said Zebediah, who had already gone through all the dresser drawers and crawled about under the bed and in the closet and generally examined the room from corner to corner. He was covered in dust bunnies because Sina is a better sculptress than housekeeper.

"Anyhow, that's how we ended up in dead Auntie

Claire's house down the road," said Winifred. "Isn't it, Wilfred?"

"Yes," said Wilfred, who reminded me a bit of Old Tom, being affable but saying little more than that which was needed at the time.

"It has four bedrooms!" Winifred went on happily. "And Mother said that that was it! This was our chance for a real home and if Daddy persisted in taking care of the *Argot* and staying in the air force instead of quitting and getting a job in Sooke—one that would allow us to live in this castle of a house we'd been left—then she would just move in there with us anyway and we would all wait for him to come to his senses. And Daddy said he didn't mind. He would continue to live on base and come down to visit when he could. Father loves the *Argot*, doesn't he, Wilfred?"

"Yes," said Wilfred.

"It's a secret spy reconnaissance plane that can fly for days without refueling," said Winifred.

"It also drops bombs," said Wilfred nonchalantly, pushing his hair out of his eyes as if he were telling us about his dog who could sit and also roll over on command.

"Because the *Argot* is so important, Daddy is a *special*

maintenance guy, making sure everything is in good working order so it can be taken out in seconds if an emergency arises," Winifred rattled on.

"What kind of emergency?" I asked.

"A war emergency, of course," said Wilfred.

"Ah, a war emergency," I said, privately thinking how unlikely *that* was.

There was military all around Vancouver Island and guns set up on strategic points around our own coastline. Ever since the start of the war, soldiers had lived in a temporary barracks on land that belonged to us but which we were lending to the war effort. At first this was very exciting, the idea that our shores would be protected from our very own farm. But despite all this vigilance, nothing much ever seemed to happen. It didn't look like the war was going to come to Vancouver Island at all, which was fine with me. Miss Macy, who was a neighbor without either job or family, liked to take long walks on our property, mostly along the coast, and visited the soldiers with Girl Guide cookies. She had told me that mostly the soldiers sat around and played poker.

"Father works every day twelve hours a day to maintain

the plane's readiness," said Winifred. "Mother says he has no time for us anymore. That he loves that plane more than he loves us."

"Which is nonsense," said Wilfred. "Mother is prone to exaggeration."

Zebediah had said not a word through all this. He had crawled back under the bed, crawled out, and pulled the mattress up to inspect the cot's springs and tried to get to the top of the highboy dresser from the chair that was stationed next to it. Now he was at the window looking out.

"What kind of garden is that?" he asked.

I joined him. "There are several. Which do you mean?" I asked.

"The one with the fence and the big lock."

"Oh," I said. "That's the night garden."

"Why do you call it the night garden?"

"Look out the window on a night when the moon is bright and find out," I said.

"Do you keep it locked to keep out the deer?" asked Zebediah.

"No," I said.

"The bears, then?" asked Wilfred.

We were all looking now.

"No."

"Well, then what?" asked Zebediah.

"I don't know," I said. "It's Old Tom who locks it."

I did know because Old Tom had once told me. But I didn't care to repeat it because it just sounded crazy.

The Maddens Settle In

ell, that first night started fine. I took them on a little tour, showing them the chicken coop and the bull pen and the cows. Then I took them to see the plow horses and I turned to Zebediah to impress upon him that he was never to get into the bull pen or in with the horses. The horses, Tag and Molly, were very sweet but very large, and accidents do happen. The bull was just mean. But when I turned, Zebediah was gone, and it took some hunting to find him climbing up the fence that surrounded the night garden and peering through.

"Did you hear what I said about the bull pen and the horses?" I asked.

"Why do you keep this fenced? There aren't any animals in it," said Zebediah.

"I told you I don't know. For heaven's sake, leave it alone. There's two hundred and seventy acres to explore; why choose the one thing that's locked up to obsess over?" But, of course, I knew that it was the fact that it *was* the one locked thing that drew him.

"Do you take care of the animals at all?" asked Winifred.

"Yes. That is, I help. Old Tom mostly takes care of the animals, and Sina does the milking. I help gather the eggs and candle them, and I help take them and the milk to Brookman's with Sina."

"Who's that?" asked Wilfred, pointing to a hunched-over figure going across one of the fields and crossing the road the military had put in that cuts through the forest to the coastal points where they had installed the big guns. I think the guns were stationed strategically to shoot at passing submarines or something, although, of course, we'd never seen a submarine. Still, it was a well-known fact that the waters around Vancouver Island were lousy with them: probably not Hitler's submarines—they were too far away—although who knew? But Russian submarines, Japanese submarines, and American submarines. I didn't know what they did, they just seemed to circle the island, but then there was so much about the war that they didn't tell us.

"That's the hermit," I said. "Sina and Old Tom let him build a cabin in the forest on our property a little way down the coast. He's probably going to the creamery to get the box of groceries Old Tom leaves for him once a week."

"You've a lot of people using your land who don't really belong here, don't you?" asked Winifred.

"I guess so," I said thoughtfully. It would have been tactless to have pointed out that this included the three of them.

"I want to see the soldiers," said Zebediah and went running toward the military road.

"Hey, come back here," I screamed.

We ran after him, and Wilfred, reaching out an arm, grabbed Zebediah's shirt collar and yanked him back the way you would a dog on a leash.

"Stop it, you idiot! You're going to get lost," said Winifred.

"He never gets lost," said Wilfred.

"Yes, actually, that's true," said Winifred. "But it's still rude to run off uninvited on someone else's property."

Zebediah didn't seem to mind. It was my guess that he was used to being yanked back by his collar and that the idea of an invitation first meant nothing to him.

Then I showed them all the beaches and coves, and before we knew it Sina had rung the dinner bell. She had installed this years before, as Old Tom and I were apt to be anywhere on the property and she didn't like yelling herself hoarse when dinner was ready.

We sat around the kitchen table eating Sina's tuna casserole, which was one of about six things she knew how to make. She had a limited but tasty repertoire. Sina's eyes kept darting from one child to the next nervously, and she later confessed to me as we did the dishes together and the Maddens took baths and unpacked that she expected one or the other of them to burst into wild sobs at any moment.

"You know," she said, "I figure nature or nurture, they had it coming and going, and surely one was bound to have caught it. The melancholic hysteria."

"No, they seem really like quite reasonable human beings," I said. "Zebediah is a bit twitchy."

"All little boys are twitchy," said Sina. "That is, if they're getting enough to eat and so have normal boy energy. I suspect all the poor starving little boys in war-torn Europe have lost their twitch, and what a sad thing that must be. But given enough food, that's what happens to a boy's energy. It all goes into the twitch. Feed them, they twitch. *Do* you think the children are getting enough food? I've never cooked for six. You don't suppose they're going to expect three meals a day, do you? I mean cooked? Should I hire a cook? You know what, I think Mrs. Brookman said her niece was staying with her and looking for employment. I'll ask when we get there tomorrow. It's very hard to be an artist and a domestic at the same time."

I was quite excited at this prospect. Sina was a good cook, but there was a certain sameness to what we ate. I had read a lot of Victorian English novels as well as spending many hammock summers skimming ancient issues of *Woman's Home Companion* that I had found in a box in the root cellar. Through them, I associated cooks with large households where there were eighteen-course dinners with pheasants and puddings and dishes with intriguing names like bubble and squeak. Where every meal was an adventure. I liked the idea of a cook and hoped the niece was at least fat; it was clear she wouldn't be old if she was Mrs. Brookman's *niece*. But cooks in Victorian novels and the stories in *Woman's*

Home Companion were always fat and old and unattractive and so devoted entirely to their kitchens. I saw puff pastry swans and Baked Alaska and other dishes that were redolent of magic coming my way. Then something dreadful occurred to me.

"She won't have to live here, too, will she?"

"Good question. I can't imagine I would want to pay anyone what it would be worth in gas to come here and back every day from Brookman's. She's apparently staying with them over the store, so conditions are quite crowded. She'd probably jump at the chance to move out. We've got the cabin we keep for the hired hands when we have them. She can have that."

"You will ask her if she can cook first, won't you?"

"I shall endeavor to do so," said Sina.

✦ ✦ ✦

After the dishes were done we gathered in the parlor and Sina played the piano and we all sang songs, songs from musicals, folk songs, hymns, and the popular songs of the day. Sina had shelves of sheet music. Winifred knew quite a few of them, as she'd been in a choir. Zebediah played the drums on the top of a side table with two pencils he'd found. It was rather annoying until Old Tom went into the kitchen and got them each a couple of spoons. Old Tom showed him how to play the spoons and they played together for a while until Zebediah tired of this, too.

"I want to go out and see the night garden at *night*," said Zebediah. "I want to climb over the fence and see what it's like inside."

Old Tom stopped playing and held Zebediah's spoons to quiet him for a moment. "The night garden is off-limits," he said simply. "You are none of you to go into it. Not ever."

"Why?" asked Zebediah.

"Never you mind," said Old Tom, and he put down his spoons, went to the couch, and began to read his newspaper.

There was an awkward silence after that, which Sina tried to fill by breaking into a rousing march on the piano, but it was too late; the happy mood of the evening could not be recovered, and in the end everyone decided to head upstairs. Sina lit the coal lanterns and distributed them. Usually Old Tom, Sina, and I liked to read for a long time in our beds before we slept. I don't know what Winifred, Wilfred, and Zebediah normally did, but they went up to their rooms as well. I decided to make one more try at my mermaid story before going to bed, so I went up to my cupola. With the advent of the Madden children I could see that I would get in little daytime writing and would have to resort to an evening schedule.

Despite that, and despite houseguests, it had certainly been successful enough, even a rather normal evening.

Then the shouting began.

The Convergence of a UFO, a Cook, and the Beginning of the Mysterious Letters

I was at my desk writing. Old Tom had gone downstairs to get some water. The Madden children were up in their rooms doing whatever they were doing. It sounded very much as if Zebediah was jumping on his bed. We may have been feeding him a bit *too* much, I was thinking, when suddenly Sina came tearing out of her room, screaming, "UFO! UFO! UFO!"

We ran downstairs after her until we were all standing on the front porch, where she was looking up into the sky, frantically turning this way and that and screaming, "UFO!" We looked up with her, but none of us could see anything except the night sky filled with stars and moon.

"Out my bedroom window!" said Sina, panting. "Out my window! I was sitting in bed reading when I heard a noise, looked up, and saw through the window over my bed something *covered* in lights, mostly blue lights, and it stopped right outside my window, that is, on the other side of the three pine trees there. And it just stood still. At first I thought it must be military. A military helicopter, because what other kind of aircraft could stay still like that? I sat there peering through the trees and wondering why in God's name it was parked right out my window and then I noticed it was really large. Large and completely stationary and I kept thinking, Why is it covered in Christmas lights? And then, from staying totally still, it took off at the speed of light. I've never seen anything move so fast. It was gone in a tic. Nothing of this earth could travel like that, from stillness to thousands of miles an hour."

"What's a UFO?" asked Zebediah.

"Unidentified flying object," said Winifred.

"Complete nonsense," said Old Tom. "No such thing."

"Well, I didn't think so before tonight either!" said Sina with exasperation. "But you can't argue with what you've *seen* with your *own two eyes*! Are you saying I *didn't* see a UFO?"

"I'm sure you saw something," said Old Tom, scratching his chin. "Some trick of light. Probably *was* a military helicopter. You said it was on the other side of the pine trees and you could only see it through the branches. Probably confused the issue."

"Don't be daft. No helicopter could move that fast," said Sina.

"Did it *sound* like a helicopter?" asked Old Tom.

"It sounded like something. I could hear it—that's what made me look up from my book. But it didn't sound like a helicopter."

"What did it sound like?" I asked.

"I don't know," said Sina. "It wasn't as *loud* as a helicopter."

"Come indoors and stop frightening the children," said Old Tom.

"I'm not frightened," said Zebediah.

"Me neither," said Wilfred.

"Maybe it was Flying Bob checking up on us," said Zebediah.

"No, Zebediah. Daddy doesn't actually fly. He just does maintenance," said Winifred.

"He *could* fly if he wanted to," said Zebediah. "He told me so."

"Yes, yes, let's all go indoors," said Old Tom.

We trooped back in, but I could see Sina didn't want to. When she saw the UFO I must have been absorbed in my mermaid story, typing away, because I hadn't seen or heard anything.

"I think we should all go back to bed. You tell us if any more Martians start spying on you," said Old Tom, chuckling.

"Stop that," snapped Sina. "I know what I saw." But then she looked a bit uncertain. "I didn't mean to snap," she added, beginning to calm down. "I know *you* didn't see it. But that doesn't change matters. I did."

"Lights play tricks at night," said Old Tom. "I'm not saying you didn't see *something*. The question is what. Could have been anything."

"It could have been Flying Bob," insisted Zebediah.

"Oh, don't be ridiculous, Zebediah," said Winifred. "It wasn't Flying Bob and it wasn't Santa Claus."

"Well, what was it?" asked Zebediah.

"Probably we'll never know," said Old Tom. "Could be Sina drifted off and dreamt it. Dreams are curious things. Sina has been known to sleepwalk."

"I wasn't asleep and I didn't dream it," said Sina and marched up to her room and slammed the door.

Old Tom raised his eyebrows and rolled his eyes at us, but instead of going back upstairs, he took his lantern and went to the couch to read. I lingered in the doorway watching him. He might have professed to be disbeliev-ing, but I noticed his eyes went to the window more than once.

✦ ✦ ✦

In the morning everyone was cheery at breakfast. Old Tom lifted his coffee cup and picked up the plate be-neath it, making circles in the air.

"What's this, then?" he asked Zebediah.

"I don't know," said Zebediah.

"Flying saucer," said Old Tom.

"Ha, ha," said Sina. "I'm going out to my studio. Franny, let me know when you have the eggs packed, and we'll put them in the truck with the milk to take to Brook-man's. I want to see about the cook while we're there."

"Can we go, too?" asked Winifred.

"All right," said Sina. "You'll have to ride in the back with the milk cans and the eggs."

"Oh boy!" said Zebediah.

"Keen," said Wilfred.

"You boys want to help me plant the potatoes while you wait for the girls?" asked Old Tom.

"Oh super boy!" said Zebediah.

"Yes, very keen," said Wilfred.

"So you think now," muttered Old Tom. "Ever plant potatoes?"

"No," said Wilfred.

"Thought not," said Old Tom, and they traipsed out to the potato field while Winifred and I cleaned up the kitchen.

We had one of those awkward moments you have when suddenly it's just the two of you and you begin to worry so hard you won't have any conversation that you don't.

"Well, jeez," I said finally when neither of us had said anything for the whole ten minutes it took to wash up.

"Yeah," said Winifred.

Then we both turned a little red.

"Say!" she said. "Is Franny short for something?"

"No," I said. "It's just, you know, Franny. Does anyone ever call you Winnie? Does anyone call Wilfred Will or Willie?"

"No," said Winifred, and she looked a bit regretful. "Daddy wanted to, but Mother said she didn't go to all the trouble picking our names just to use some ugly short version. She said once you start that you never get back to the long version."

"Well," I said, considering. "That's probably true."

"I suppose you could call me Winnie until we leave," said Winifred. "If that's what you prefer."

"Oh, I have no preferences about what I call you until you leave. When," I asked trickily, "do you suppose that will be?"

"I don't know. Mother didn't say. I know she is worried about Daddy doing something stupid, but she didn't say what. She didn't really tell us much of anything."

"Didn't you want to ask?"

"Mother is a worrier. She always thinks everyone is going to do something catastrophic, but they never do. As soon as she figures out Daddy is okay, she'll be back."

"Oh well," I said. "Let's go get the eggs."

We ran down to the chicken coop. There are cooperative hens and uncooperative hens. I schooled Winifred on how to approach them and which ones were liable to give her a hard time; nevertheless, the first time one of them flew at her and pecked, she went shrieking from the chicken coop and stood outside the door continuing to shriek hysterically. I wondered if this were her yet-unseen Crying Alice side. Mind you, we've all had our bad chicken days.

"What a horrid, horrid bird," she said when she got her breath.

I regarded the one who had gone for her levelly and said, "Yes, and I'll show you what we do with horrid birds." I approached the hen, grabbed it authoritatively by the ankles, and put it into a cage at the corner of the coop.

"Is that to keep it from pecking people?" she asked, coming back into the coop hesitantly.

"Sort of," I said. "I'm supposed to pick the worst layer every week and put it in the cage, and that's Sunday supper. But, secretly, I put the one who is giving me the most trouble there."

"I don't think I can eat it," said Winifred. "It's a bit like not just taking no prisoners but *eating* your enemies."

"I imagine you'll change your mind when you smell Old Tom's Sunday chicken. But never mind. Let's candle and pack the eggs."

Winifred and I went into the egg candling room on the side of the coop. She turned out to be an excellent egg candler once I showed her how to look for blood or meat spots by holding the egg in front of the light of the egg candler. She found several eggs with ominous spots and we packed them separately. Those were the eggs we kept at home because Sina said they were just fine to eat if you weren't so terribly squeamish about these things. Winifred didn't break a single egg. Then we went in to get washed before going to Brookman's. I followed her upstairs. She had blood from the pecking on her shirt and wanted to change.

"I'll be in the cupola," I said. "Call me when you're ready to go."

I need to check in there fairly often. Not to write, not to look for whales with my telescope, but just to be in there, the room where things might *happen*. As if I can go in there and feel those things *waiting*.

"What's up there?" asked Winifred. "Can I come up and see before I change?"

"No, I'm very sorry, but no one is allowed. It's where I write."

"Oh," said Winifred. She thought about this and then asked, "Can I read something you've finished writing?"

"Well, I haven't exactly managed that part yet."

"How do you know you can, then?" she asked.

"I don't. That's what's so frustrating. But you have to try."

This reminded me of Old Tom's Church of Lost Causes, but I couldn't possibly believe it was a lost cause or why bother?

"Why don't you write about Sina's UFO?" she suggested.

That's the problem with telling people you write. They always want to give you things to write about. As if the things you write about could come from them. Or from you.

"Gee, shouldn't you get changed?" I said.

"You don't want to talk about it anymore," she said kindly, and ran off to change and wasn't all huffy the way she could have been had she misinterpreted my reticence as snottiness. Probably living with Crying Alice had inured her to strange people.

As I went up the stairs I had a sudden idea. I wrote *Church of Lost Causes* on a piece of typing paper and I took a chair and scotch-taped it over the door outside the cupola. It made me feel vaguely better, as if I had done the opposite of jinxing things. I had taken the pressure off. If it was a lost cause, if it was celebrated, worshipped as a lost cause, then maybe something could sneak in and happen after all.

I heard Winifred come into the hall, so I ran down to join her and we went out to Sina's studio.

Sina was staring at the sculpture she had made. It was a mermaid and it was quite beautiful, I thought, but as we stood there she kicked it over and jumped on it with both feet.

"Botheration," she said. "I'm going to give up. I'm simply going to give up. I always wanted to sculpt in marble. Michelangelo—now, *there's* an artist."

"Well, why don't you?" asked Winifred.

"I tried. I can't. Clay is my medium. But real sculptors use marble. The *David*, *there's* a statue. The *Pietà*, nice bit of work. The *Prisoners*, *genius*. *Genius*. The prisoners trying to get out of the marble. But nothing tries to get out of my clay. It sits there like a lump. I give up. I'm going to get a job as a waitress."

Then she stomped into the house to rinse off, calling, "Load up the truck, girls," over her shoulder.

"Oh dear," said Winifred. "Mother said that Sina's semi-famous. She said there is a piece of hers outside the Parliament Building in downtown Victoria. Is she really going to quit sculpting?"

"I doubt it. She says that every day. Your mother may think she's famous, but Sina never likes anything she's finished. She says it never lives up to its potential. Even the piece outside Parliament."

"She lives in artistic torment," said Winifred.

Really, for someone who did not come from an artistic family, Winifred had a good grasp of the matter. Or perhaps she was simply a good listener.

We carefully carried the egg flats and put them in the back of the truck with the milk cans. Then we ran to the potato field to get the boys. Wilfred had a bag of seed potatoes and was working diligently alongside Old Tom planting. Zebediah was running up and down the rows with his arms outstretched going *bzzzzzz* with his lips.

"Zebediah, stop being a plane. Come on, it's time to go," called Winifred.

"You'd think he'd rather be called just Will," I said in low tones to Winifred, thinking Wilfred wouldn't hear me.

But he did. He put down his hoe and said, "You can call me Will."

"What do you want to be called, boy?" asked Old Tom. "Don't let those girls railroad you."

"I don't really care," said Wilfred.

"That's the spirit," said Old Tom. "It never matters what people call you. Hoe your own row. Run your own race. Stay in your own lane." He nodded his head decidedly and went back to planting.

"I wouldn't railroad him," I called over my shoulder to Old Tom as we raced to the truck.

"I know that," Old Tom called back.

But it was now clear to me that it was too late to

impose nicknames on these three. I would have to content myself with the splendid nicknames of their parents.

"Bzzzzz," said Zebediah with his arms still outstretched, jumping over the fence that surrounded the potato field. *"Bzzzzzz."*

"He's obsessed with flying," said Winifred.

The boys were splotched with dirt from the field, but that didn't seem to bother them.

We found seats in the back of the truck on benches Old Tom had put there.

"Mind the eggs and don't sit on any," said Winifred.

Then Sina came out of the house and jumped into the driver's seat dressed in her going-to-Brookman's best. She always wore a dress and her good hat. You never knew who you were going to see at Brookman's.

Once we got there we took the eggs and milk around to the back to give them to Mrs. Brookman; then we went around again and came in the front door. Mrs. Brookman paid Sina, and out of that Sina gave us each a nickel for a chocolate bar. This involved a long, careful survey of available options while on the other side of the room Sina and the six ladies who were there gossiped and drank coffee as the radio played in the background. All of a sudden Sina shrieked, reached over, and turned up the dial. It was the local news and the announcer was saying, "A fast-flying blue light was seen by Victorians in last night's sky. And the Canadian Space Institute has asked anyone who saw last night's blue light to call them immediately. The Canadian Space Institute says they believe it to have been a meteor."

"That's my meteor! That's my meteor!" cried Sina, leaping up and down. "I saw it! I saw the blue light!"

"Did you now, dear?" said Mrs. Brookman. "Well, you must use my phone and call the Space Institute."

"Yes, you must!" said another of the ladies. "It's your duty."

"It's practically a patriotic duty," said Miss Macy, who, because she lived alone, came to Brookman's quite a bit for the company. "Do we know what the evil enemy nations have come up with to torment us? It could be a German or a Japanese meteor!"

Sina and Mrs. Brookman looked at Miss Macy with pity. It was a well-known fact that she was a bit wanting.

"Meteors have no nationality. They can't be *corralled,* dear," said Mrs. Brookman to her gently. "Meteors are, well, wild. They're feral. Like wolves."

"Oh, I see," said Miss Macy. "Still, we've all been told to watch for enemy submarines, haven't we? I suspect that extends to space. Objects from space. Enemy objects from space."

"Call, call," urged the ladies, ignoring Miss Macy.

So with great self-importance and a certain triumph in having seen both something unusual and something Space Institute–worthy, and more than a little pleased to be vindicated, Sina stepped up to the phone while we all fell silent. She picked up the receiver and dialed.

"Hello?" she said. "Yes, well, I saw the blue light. Yes, the, uh, meteor. Yes, I did, I saw the blue meteor they mentioned on the radio. Mrs. Whitekraft. In Sooke. The East Sooke Farm. Yes, oh, you would? Why? All right, yes, I guess that would be fine. Say two o'clock? Right you are. Very good. You're welcome."

She hung up and turned to us beaming. "They want to *interview* me!" she said proudly.

"Well, I never," said one of the ladies. "You'll probably be part of research."

"You'll probably be part of history!" said Miss Macy, who always took things one step too far.

"At least you'll know you've done your duty," said Mrs. Brookman.

"Why don't *I* ever get to see any meteors?" asked Miss Macy.

"How could it be a meteor when it just hung there outside your window?" asked Wilfred. But no one was paying him any attention. Nobody ever paid attention to children when there were grown-ups in the room. It was one of the wonderful things about being a child. It was like being invisible. I knew I would rue the day when I was grown up and accountable and taken seriously.

"I must bustle home," said Sina, who was already making bustly movements, so excited was she. "The parlor needs dusting and I should make some tea cookies or something in case the man from the Space Institute expects it. Oh, *drat*. I don't know how to make cookies. Mrs. Brookman, I almost forgot that I wanted to ask if that niece of yours is still about."

Mrs. Brookman set her lips and nodded grimly.

"I wonder if I might borrow her for as long as we are hosting the Madden children? I need a cook. I am prepared to pay. Does she cook, your niece?"

"Oh yes!" said Mrs. Brookman. "Cooks up a treat. Gladys, get out here."

Gladys was apparently skulking about the back room because she appeared through the curtained doorway two seconds later. I had my doubts about her. For one thing, as

I've said, in books cooks were older women, so she seemed awfully young. Her look was all wrong as well. She wasn't fat, as she should have been, but slim with a lot of frizzy blond hair and a lot of makeup. More makeup than you generally saw women wearing in these parts. And her dress was unkempt and yet the latest fashion. That's something else you didn't often see around here. All of us girls at school knew the latest fashions and passed about pictures from catalogs and such when we had them, but nobody we knew, not our teachers or mothers or the ladies at Brookman's, used to making do since the war, ever dressed in these fashionable clothes. But here was someone with a fashionable dress, something many of us would have given our eyeteeth for, and yet she hadn't bothered to keep it nice. Had it been any of us girls, lucky enough to own a dress like that, we would have kept it clean and pressed, in mint condition hanging in the closet and brought it out only on the most special of occasions. The casual way with which Gladys treated it, well, there was just something not very nice about it. In fact, there was just something not quite right about Gladys. You could tell at first glance. And she was grubby. There was at least a good week's accumulation of dirt under her fingernails, and her hair didn't look like it had been brushed in a while; there was a ratty bit sticking up at the back. All in all, she didn't look like someone you'd want messing around with your food.

"Gladys, Mrs. Whitekraft is here to offer you a job."

"Must be a mistake," said Gladys, turning and heading back behind the curtained doorway. "Because I didn't apply for none."

"Get back out here, Gladys. It's your lucky day. You didn't *apply* for none—uh, one—but one has been offered to you. Mrs. Whitekraft needs a cook. You can cook."

"No I can't," said Gladys.

"Yes you can. I've seen you," said Mrs. Brookman.

"You'd live on our farm, of course. For the duration. It isn't a permanent position. You'd have your own cabin. It's reasonably nice," said Sina, her eyes getting a little vague and uncertain about this last bit.

"There's an outhouse," said Zebediah encouragingly. "With bats."

Zebediah was very taken with the outhouse. Luckily he was still being ignored.

"Well, I don't know. I'm happy here," said Gladys stubbornly. "I'm not sure I could work a cooking job into my schedule, you see."

For this last, Gladys developed a snooty upper-class

tone that was meant to intimidate but just made her sound like she was doing bad theater.

"Nonsense," said Mrs. Brookman. "Your mother sent you here to broaden your horizons. So, uh, broad. Er, broaden. Go cook."

"It's very broadening," said Miss Macy in her usual dreamy tone. Miss Macy could be elated about anything because facts and real life never got in her way. "Oh, the stews I have known! The chilies! One word of advice, dear," she said, grabbing Gladys's arms confidingly, causing Gladys to back across the room and into a wall. "Make bread your friend!"

"Yikes, keep her away from me," said Gladys, who had airs but no social graces.

"Run along and pack your things. You can start immediately. We must give our all for the military effort." Mrs. Brookman had her by the shoulders and was practically shoving her in the direction of the living quarters.

"I don't see how being a cook for some farmer is helping the military," said Gladys.

"Farmers are the backbone of the nation," said Miss Macy. "They grow the food for our boys overseas."

As if to punctuate this, Miss Macy came to attention with a clicking of heels that would have been smarter had she not been wearing orthopedic shoes. She saluted, necessitating everyone saluting back. Which gave me an idea.

"We've got the military on our property!" I said.

Of course, no one paid any attention to me, but something of what I said must have penetrated Sina's realm of grown-up consciousness because she said, "You'll never guess, but on our property we have troops stationed in barracks. The soldiers just walking all over the place."

"I'll pack my bags," said Gladys. She turned and went through the curtained doorway and upstairs to get her things. A minute later she was back wearing high heels that would last about two seconds on the farm and lines drawn down the back of her legs the way girls did when they couldn't afford nylons. Only Gladys's were squiggly and badly drawn, so it looked as if her nylons were sagging and she needed to pull them up. I was to learn that this was a trademark of Gladys's from her appearance to her cooking: everything was kind of randomly half-done as if she *could* do better but couldn't be bothered. She dragged a heavy suitcase behind her.

"I hope I can impress upon you that my duties can't be tooooo taxing?" she said to Sina, using her fake snooty accent again as we walked out to the truck. "I need lots of time for my mystical fine tunings?"

Gladys climbed into the cab of the truck to sit on the upturned milk can that we used for a passenger seat and Winifred, Wilfred, Zebediah, and I climbed into the back.

"Your *what*?" asked Sina.

"My mystical fine tunings? I'm a psychic?" she said. Gladys dropped the snooty accent and took up the equally annoying habit of ending all her sentences on a high note as if they were questions. I was busily punctuating them in my head, and I wanted to give her a short lesson in the art of the declarative, but I knew Sina was itching to do it herself. Of course neither one of us would be so rude.

"I plan to make a living of it? You know, predictions, tea leaves, aura readings? Right now I'm studying crystal balls. I got a gift where balls are concerned."

"Oh really," said Sina drily. "It is always so comforting to believe in something, isn't it? Old Tom once had an aunt who believed in leprechauns. And the people in Iceland believe in elves. They must derive so much comfort from that tripe. Hang on to the door there on the curves; that milk can is none too steady."

Sina started the truck.

"Can you read my fortune?" yelled Zebediah.

"Oh yes," said Gladys. "Your aura is very strong. Have you got a quarter?"

"I don't have any money," said Zebediah.

"I feel my powers fading," said Gladys.

We were about to pull away when Mrs. Brookman came running out, calling, "Dear, I almost forgot your mail!" She rushed up to Sina's window and passed her a pile of letters, and we headed home.

Once at the farm, Sina helped Gladys get settled into the cabin and then tried to convince her to make tea cookies, but Gladys said that her powers of divination were telling her that it was not an auspicious day for baking.

"Stuff and nonsense," said Sina. "Do as you're told."

"All right," said Gladys sulkily, getting off the cot in the cabin where she had collapsed with one of the beauty magazines she'd brought with her. "But I can take no responsibility for what happens as a result."

"Can we look at your beauty magazines while you bake?" Winifred and I asked, but Gladys only glared at us and locked the cabin door with the key Sina had given her.

"She's not very friendly," whispered Winifred.

Sina showed Gladys the kitchen. Wilfred had gone back out to help Old Tom where he was planting peas, lettuce, carrots, beets, and runner beans in the kitchen garden. Zebediah, Winifred, and I just traipsed around after Sina because we didn't want to miss the appearance of the Space Institute man. Sina had settled in the parlor and was sorting through the mail when, looking up at us, she suddenly said, "Oh." Mrs. Brookman had given her the Maddens' mail to hold until Crying Alice got back. Sina took a letter from the Maddens' pile and handed it to Zebediah. "*This* one's for you," she said. "Now shoo. I've got bills to pay, and if you distract me, I'll put the checks in all the wrong envelopes. I've done it before and it takes forever to sort out."

"Will you call us when the space man comes?" asked Zebediah.

"Sure. Now shoo," said Sina again, but instead of bill paying she began nervously dusting and straightening the parlor.

We went out to sit on the porch steps.

"Who's it from?" asked Winifred, trying to grab the letter out of Zebediah's hands to see for herself, but he clutched it to him.

"Let go, it's mine!" he said.

"Well, open it, then," demanded Winifred.

"No," said Zebediah.

"Don't you want to know who it's from?" asked Winifred.

"I already know. And it's secret. I'm *sworn* to secrecy."

"Nonsense," said Winifred. "You're just trying to make yourself important. You'd better let me read it. It might have big words."

"He promised it wouldn't," said Zebediah.

"Who promised? Is it from Daddy?" demanded Winifred in outraged tones. "Is he writing to *you* and not to us?"

"It's none of your business," said Zebediah, and then when Winifred started to stand up to try to grab the letter, he leapt off the porch and made for the woods.

"Let him go," said Winifred wearily.

Watching him run, I surmised we had no choice. For someone with such short little legs, he ran like the wind and was across the fields and under cover of the forest before we knew it.

"Are you sure he won't get lost?" I asked. "He may have a good sense of direction, but it's a big forest."

"Doesn't matter. I think he has a compass in his

brain," said Winifred. "And there's no sense trying to get something away from him that he doesn't want to give you. He's got a terrible stubborn streak. Mother says he gets it from Daddy. You can never tell Daddy what to do or what not to do either. Anyhow, I'll just sneak into his room some night and read it. Daddy is probably just sending him drawings of planes or something. They're both plane crazy. They're both plain *crazy*." She laughed heartily at her own joke but stopped when a car suddenly came barreling toward the house. When it pulled up we could see it was a very important-looking little man with a fedora and a lot of pens and small instruments in his shirt pocket.

"It must be . . ." said Winifred.

I looked at him breathlessly. "The man from the Space Institute."

The Man from the
Space Institute

ina," I yelled, running into the house, "it's the man from the Space Institute! He's here!"

"He's here two hours early," said Sina grumpily, emerging from the parlor.

We went to the kitchen to see how the cookies were coming, but Gladys was sitting on the kitchen table singing bits of bebop and hitting her leg with a spoon in time to the music in her head. There was flour everywhere, and there were ashes from the stove drifting about.

"Cookies?" asked Sina.

"Rome wasn't built in a day," said Gladys mysteriously and went on tapping her leg.

Sina sighed and we went back to meet the scientist.

"Oh well, he can't expect cookies if he comes two hours early. He's probably a physicist. They don't believe in time. Where is he?"

I pointed to the front porch, where he had made his way and was chatting to Winifred.

"Hello," said Sina, coming out and shaking his hand. "Do come in."

"Long way out here. Winding roads," said the scientist, grabbing her hand and shaking it enthusiastically and then wiping his forehead as if he'd just come off the Oregon Trail. He took his shoes off on the porch with such wrist flicks and exaggerated motions as if to make clear this was not ordinary good manners but Space Institute protocol, infusing the occasion with ceremony and import along the lines of surgeons scrubbing up before an operation. Sina wasn't a stickler for indoor shoe removal, and the rest of us had our shoes on, but we didn't point this out. We felt a man from the Space Institute must certainly know what he was doing. We children watched in awe, as if we'd never seen anyone remove their shoes before, and then we all went inside.

"Well," said Sina, "take heart. I think cookies may eventually be forthcoming."

Smoke was issuing from the kitchen and we could hear Gladys shouting, "*Dadblastit!* I hate this woodstove!"

"Or perhaps not," said Sina. "Do come into the parlor."

"Actually," said the man, "I'd like to see the window from which you saw the meteor."

"Why?" asked Sina, looking panicked, and I knew what she was thinking. She'd managed to straighten up the parlor and dust. But Sina's bedroom was always total squalor.

"I'd like to take measurements," said the man. "If you don't mind."

Sina looked like she did mind but couldn't think of a reason to say no.

"Can we come?" asked Winifred.

"Yes, yes, that is, I *think* so," said Sina absently, no doubt trying to remember just how bad things were up there and whether it was fit for young eyes. "Where's Zebediah? Didn't he want to meet the Space Institute man, too?"

"Mr. Hastings," said the man, tipping his fedora.

"He's run off," said Winifred. "We don't know where."

"Well, I hope he's not with the pigs," said Sina. "Boys

always seem to gravitate to the thing that can make them dirtiest and cause the most trouble."

Mr. Hastings laughed amiably, which startled Sina because she hadn't thought she'd been making a joke.

"What about Wilfred?" asked Sina.

"He's with Old Tom," I said.

Sina stuck her head out the window and called, "Wilfred! The man from the Space Institute is here!"

But Old Tom and Wilfred each just batted a hand in her direction as if to say, Yeah, yeah, doing important things here, leave us alone.

"Birds of a feather," said Sina. "Well, come along."

We trooped upstairs. Sina approached the door to her room as if it might be rigged with a bomb. She gently, gently prized it open and peeked in.

"Um," she said, "perhaps I'd better just give it a quick tidy."

"Oh, no need, we of the Space Institute see all sorts of things," said Mr. Hastings, anxious to get on with it.

But Sina put her hand on his steadily advancing chest and gave him a firm push backward, which seemed to surprise him. She took advantage of his surprise and slipped into her room, closing and locking the door behind her. We heard a lot of furious activity and now and then, I'm afraid, an uttered oath. When she finally opened the door, she was flushed with the tumult of her action, her hair was in wisps about her sweaty face, and there was a long green sock dangling from her gray bun. I reached behind her and swiftly yanked it off and dropped it behind my back. Sina hadn't noticed and she smiled graciously at Mr. Hastings as if none of this had happened and said, "Do come in."

Gazing around, I wondered what it must have looked like before Sina's quick tidy because there were still newspapers strewn about. Sina liked to read them in bed. The bed wasn't made and there was an apple core and a bunch of dirty Kleenexes in the middle of it. Clothes were lying about in piles as if being sorted for the laundry, as, indeed, they probably were. Sina liked to keep three piles going: dirty, almost-dirty-enough-to-wash-but-still-wearable, and clean-but-not-yet-folded. She'd explained the piles to me a long time ago and said she wasn't recommending it, only explaining it. Now her face became blank and it was clear she had decided the best thing was to brazen her way through and make no apologies, because she got down to business immediately and said, "I saw it out that window right there." She pointed to the window over her bed.

"Interesting," said Mr. Hastings, taking some instruments out of his shirt pocket. "Do you mind?" He gestured that he wanted to get on the bed.

Sina held her hands out in the manner of a duchess saying Be my guest, and he crawled across the bed, also pretending the dirty Kleenexes and apple core weren't there, and began measuring various angles.

"And where did you see it exactly out the window?"

"Um," she said, "it was there. Just through those trees."

"Interesting," he said again. "Did you see it as a . . ."—Mr. Hastings paused dramatically and turned his head slowly to look her in the eye and finish meaningly—"*blue light?*"

Winifred and I jumped, but Sina stoically kept both feet on the floor.

"Yes," lied Sina, her face beginning to twitch in its characteristic tell because, of course, she'd already told us it had lots of blinking lights, only some of them blue. "Yes, I did. That's why I called. Because on the radio they said it cast . . ." And here her dramatic pause answered his and she copied his slow head turn and piercing look. *"A blue light."*

"Quite," said Mr. Hastings.

He looked at Sina searchingly. Although they had several feet between them, they seemed to be locked in some kind of dance, moving to the silent beat of what they would not say.

"This blue light—I mean, this obvious *meteor* . . ."

He was asking for something, but Sina just blushed and looked down.

"We *are* talking about a *meteor* . . ." he said, and even though it was a statement, it seemed to hold a question.

"Yes," said Sina so breathlessly we could hardly hear her. I was sure at that point she was on the verge of confession.

"How fast would you say it was going? Did it appear to be making its way to the horizon . . . with . . ." Again the pause, again the head turn, again the piercing eyes. "Speed?"

Winifred and I leaned forward involuntarily, so as not to miss a word.

"Oh," she said. "Well, speed, speed is a, uh *tricky thing*."

"Ah," he said, nodding as if seriously considering the matter. "That's what we're talking about, then, is it? A tricky thing."

"Tricky," agreed Sina.

"Hmmm," said Mr. Hastings. Then, still balanced

precariously on his knees on the saggy mattress, he silently measured and remeasured what I was sure he had measured properly the first time. I got the impression he was stalling, giving her a chance to come clean, but Sina remained stoically silent.

"This meteor seemed to move with *consistent* speed?" he asked at last, changing his tactic, and appearing nonchalant as if he didn't really care about the meteor although it had been clear before that he hung on Sina's every word. I had the feeling that he didn't believe a word she said and was hoping to thus crack her open.

Sina, borrowing from Crying Alice, said, "Well, it appeared contiguous."

This seemed to stump Mr. Hastings, who wrote something down. Perhaps, *Subject has less than perfect command of the English language.*

"So is there anything else?" he asked.

"Should there be?" countered Sina.

"Excuse me," said Winifred, breaking the spell in the little dance of that-of-which-we-do-not-speak. "But what exactly were you measuring?"

"Angles," he said smiling at her. "Always . . . the angles."

He hissed this last, causing Winifred and me to back up several paces and nod frantically as if we hoped by doing so we could fend off any attacks when he finally went completely off his nut.

"Angles, yes, angles," we parroted. Even though this really didn't elucidate anything, we thought it best to agree enthusiastically.

Why, I wondered, was nothing that was being thought being said? Why was Sina, so insistent with her family that she'd seen a UFO, refusing to divulge it to the one person prepared to believe her? Mr. Hastings seemed to be wondering the same thing as he stayed kneeling, leaning closer and closer to her as she stood at the edge of the bed unmoving, as if mesmerized by his professional Space Institute hypnotic gaze. He stared more and more deeply into her eyes. Who would blink first? Well, Mr. Hastings, it turned out because in the silence he leaned forward bit by bit until the mattress, which had been doing its sorry saggy best to support him, gave up and collapsed to one side and he fell off the bed with a crash. I had to hand it to him because he got up unapologetically, looking none the worse for wear, just brushing off his pants a bit, as if falling off beds were standard operating procedure for they of the Space Institute. Now that the spell of trying to draw from Sina that-of-which-she-would-not-speak was broken, he became all cheerful and normal, just your run-of-the-mill, dull fuddy-duddy scientist and said, "Well, we appreciate you calling. If you think of anything else to tell us will you call again?"

"Yes, of course," said Sina as, with some relief, we vacated her room and she closed the door.

"What time did you say this was?" Mr. Hastings asked casually, as if it were an afterthought, which it clearly wasn't, while we trotted downstairs again. "That you saw it?"

"Oh, I don't know, around nine-thirty, wouldn't you say, Franny?" asked Sina, who had likewise gotten all normal and businesslike again. You'd think *her* world couldn't possibly contain things as mysterious and magical as UFOs and strange knowing men from the Space Institute.

"Yes, around that," I said.

We escorted Mr. Hastings to the front porch, where he put his shoes back on without any of the ceremony he had used to take them off. I wondered whether, had Sina told him the real story of the UFO, he would have returned his shoes to his Space Institute feet with an evidence-finding ceremony all its own. It was very sad that we would never know.

Because we could think of nothing more to say, a kind of pregnant pause ensued. I'd never experienced a pregnant pause before—that is, a silence so full of something about to happen that it's as if there is an invisible living thing, the embryo of an event, within it. It was an interesting experience.

Then, as he straightened up to leave, Mr. Hastings suddenly turned and looked Sina right in the eye and said, "It's a good thing you didn't think it was . . ."—and here his gaze once more became intense—"a UFO!"

At this we all jumped. We couldn't help it. But when Sina froze and still said nothing, he began to laugh jovially as if it had all been in good fun.

"Hahahaha," he went on amiably, but his eyes were not amiable; they were beady little lasers, piercing into Sina's, asking but not asking and I was about to say, That's exactly what she *did* think, if just to put an end to this stand-off, but was stopped before I began by Sina also laughing amiably and saying, "Yes, good thing," and then looking quickly away.

Mr. Hastings gave her one last searching glance and said, "Good-bye." A word that was suddenly rife with meaning.

"Good-bye," said Sina, equally meaningly, and herded us inside before closing the door.

I turned to her and said, "You're right! It *was* a UFO! And he *knew*! He *knew* it was a UFO!"

"Hush," said Sina, hustling us toward the kitchen as we heard the car pull away.

Gladys had apparently given up on the cookies. There were trays of little burnt nuggets scattered around the kitchen and no Gladys in sight. Sina sat us down at the kitchen table and put on the kettle. She always recovered from things with a pot of tea.

"He was fishing!" I said. "He knew you hadn't seen a meteor. He wanted you to say it without putting words in your mouth."

"Yes," said Sina. "I believe you're right. I'm an idiot. The trouble is, when I talked to the Space Institute on the phone at Brookman's I said I'd seen 'the meteor' and somehow I didn't feel I could backtrack from that without looking a fool. It's 'The Emperor's New Clothes' all over again. I have no moral courage."

And before the water even got a chance to boil she stood up, turned, and stomped upstairs.

"Where are you going?" I called after her.

"To clean my room," she said and we could hear her slamming things about up there, so we took the kettle off the stove and went outside to find Zebediah. Winifred suggested we look in the woods for him and tell him his secretiveness with his letter had caused him to miss the Space Institute man. She was feeling quite gleeful about this.

"It was the way Mr. Hastings *said* it," I explained to Winifred as we were walking. "He was trying to get her to admit it was a UFO. He was testing her."

"Why didn't he just come out and ask?" Winifred said. "I mean, if he *knew* that's what it was?"

"Because if they go around asking people if they've seen any UFOs lately, then suddenly people think they've seen things they haven't or they want to appear important so they make things up they didn't see. I think people have to come to *them* with what they saw; the Space Institute men can't just tell them it was a UFO and go from there. I don't even think he was taking measurements. I mean, what kind of measurements could those possibly have been? I think he was just trying to give her a chance to spill the beans."

"Sina should call them back."

"Maybe she will," I said. But somehow I knew she

wouldn't. That this whole demoralizing incident had capped her glorious UFO experience in a way that couldn't be uncapped. It was embarrassing enough to tell people who didn't believe you what you'd seen. But to *not* tell someone who was prepared to believe you was far worse.

Then to my astonishment we saw Zebediah with the hermit. They were coming down the coastal path that Old Tom had made years ago. The hermit, as far as I knew, hadn't talked to anyone since his accident except for Old Tom. And even then not so much because, Old Tom says, the hermit has only part of his wits and sometimes forgets even how to talk and has to use hand gestures. Old Tom figures the hermit had a terrible blow to the head and too much exposure to cold waters before managing to crawl up out of the ocean, and it left him permanently wanting.

"What were you doing with the hermit?" I asked as Zebediah came running up to us and the hermit turned back for home.

"I was spying on him," said Zebediah. "Through the trees. His house is made of driftwood and is set back in the woods away from the path. You would never know it was there if you didn't know how to find it. I found it exploring a deer trail. He's got a pulley that goes down to the beach to bring up anything he finds beachcombing. He's got his own vegetable garden. He saw me and asked me in."

"He asked you in?" I said, further astonished. "He's never said word one to me."

"That's so Zebediah," said Winifred. "You just go and insinuate yourself everywhere, don't you?"

"What's his place like on the inside?" I asked. I had spied on it, too, from time to time but had never been inside.

"He's got millions of books," said Zebediah.

"That's very odd," I said. "Because he never goes to town, so how would he get them?"

"The hermit told me that Old Tom gives them to him."

"I didn't know," I said, feeling a bit put out that the hermit was telling Zebediah things that he and Old Tom hadn't told me. I mean, the hermit didn't talk to people at all, but it seemed to me that if he did he should talk to me, not Zebediah, since, after all, he was on our property. I realized uncomfortably that this made it seem as if I thought we, in some sense, owned the hermit and it wasn't that exactly, but really it was galling that the hermit preferred confiding in a twitchy six-year-old boy rather than a charming, clever twelve-year-old girl.

"How did he get here?" asked Winifred.

"Old Tom says he was wearing the remnants of what looked like a very tattered air force uniform when he found him one day peacefully building a shelter in the woods. When Old Tom told him he was only another three kilometers to our house the hermit said nothing. So then Old Tom asked the hermit if he had been in the air force and had an accident, but the hermit didn't remember what branch of the military he'd been in or what exactly had happened. Old Tom figured he had somehow washed up on shore, so Old Tom walked the cliff trail back and forth for days to make sure no one else was lying hurt and needing rescue. He offered to help the hermit find family or call the air force for him, but the hermit begged Old Tom not to tell anyone about him. He was afraid they would take him away. He loved the cabin he was building. Old Tom said from the construction of it you could tell he was smart and had all kinds of skills. He also said it's unlikely that anyone who stumbled on him would take note but it's just as well his cabin was tucked back in the forest.

"Old Tom said it was fine with him if the hermit

didn't want anyone to know about him. He's not keeping it a secret exactly; he's just not announcing his presence. Old Tom figured that the hermit had done his time in the service of his country. And it had clearly taken something from him and we owed it to him to let him build a safe haven for himself. So Old Tom bought him a pile of clothes and brought him pots and pans and blankets and things to make him more comfortable, a little at a time so as not to overwhelm him. And he made him a deal that he would give him vegetable plants to start his own garden, and vegetables until it was ready, along with milk, butter, and eggs and periodically a little flour and sugar and such and leave it all in a box in the creamery every week. And in return the hermit would have to do something for him. Something Old Tom said he couldn't do himself. And he agreed."

"What did he want the hermit to do?" asked Zebediah.

"Weed the night garden," I said.

And then the dinner bell rang.

THE FIRST LETTER

We were all sitting around the dining room table. We had had to make the move to these swankier quarters because with Gladys there were definitely too many people to fit around our small kitchen table. Sina had put huge candelabras on the heavy old wood table, saving the coal oil for lighting later. It felt very regal. We never sat there, Sina and Old Tom and I. Usually the table just got used if Sina and Old Tom wanted to spread out the egg and milk records and figure out what the heck was going on with the paperwork. But now we were sitting around it like royalty, and with the candelabras burning bright, I thought my potential friend's comment of "strangely medieval" to be suddenly apropos. It was such a large table that in order to pass things to each other, we had to get up and take a few steps, that or send the bowls flying along the boards like china luges and hope for the best. In front of us was burnt fish, burnt potatoes, and burnt green beans. There were burnt cookies for dessert.

"The trouble is," said Gladys, when she noticed us staring forlornly at this burnt bacchanalia, not knowing where to begin, "apart from that stupid stove—and I might add that nobody where I come from, in a civilized town like Nanaimo, would still be cooking on a wood-burning stove—apart from that, the trouble is that I've nothing to distract me while I cook."

"I would hate to see what would happen if you *were* distracted," said Sina.

"No, no, you see that's exactly what you *do* want. Because the part of my brain that works best is not the concentrating part."

"Evidently," said Old Tom, still trying to make a go of his burnt potatoes. Old Tom loved potatoes. He looked as if he couldn't believe someone had finally stumbled on a way to make potatoes inedible.

"The part of my brain that works is the back part. You know the part back of my head," Gladys went on in the happy way people who like to talk about themselves do. This caused us all to look at the prominent rats' nest tangle of at least a week's vintage residing there.

Gladys lifted a fork and waved it idly around over her hair as she spoke so that little bits of burnt salmon dropped into it. We were all getting an idea of how she came to be so unkempt, because she made no effort to get the fish bits out again. There was a pink salmon chunk sticking up and because it was on top of her head it looked like some brain had come poking through to hear her lecture on the parts of it. It mesmerized us. We just kept staring. Zebediah giggled.

Gladys gave him a look that would have withered a lesser person and said, "You see, people, they either have the back or the front part of their brain working. Never both. And if you've got the back part, well, then it's no good trying to do stuff with the front. Because it will never work. It will just make a mess. It will just burn the fish. The thing you have to do is distract the front so you can work with the back. Great cooks use the back. Artists use the back. Psychics, that is to say me, use the back."

"Who uses the front?" asked Wilfred, blinking inquisitively behind his large lenses.

"Factory workers," said Gladys.

"I want to be a factory worker when I grow up," said Winifred, surprising all of us and making us sit up a bit, tilting our heads at her inquiringly.

"Really? What kind of factory?" I asked, happy to get off the subject of Gladys's brain.

"I don't care," said Winifred.

"I believe that's the first time I've ever heard anyone say that," said Sina, continuing to stare at Winifred tilt-headed. I could see Winifred had gone up in her estimation.

"When we were in grade four we had to pick what we wanted to be when we grew up and make a poster. When I said factory worker everyone laughed, but I didn't care. I made one rule for myself and that is never to pretend to be something I'm not."

"That's very admirable, dear," said Sina. "And very liberating, I would think. I'm sure you'll be a heck of a factory worker."

"We're getting off the subject of how to distract the front part of my brain," said Gladys, sullenly pushing her burnt food away.

"Uh-huh," said Sina, who had given up and put cornflakes and milk on the table and was passing out bowls. "And how do you propose doing that?"

"I'm glad you asked," said Gladys, perking up. "A radio would work a treat. I could listen to it with the front part of my brain, and that would distract it enough to get the back part going."

"No," said Sina.

"You might at least give it a try," said Gladys.

"No," said Sina. "I won't have one of those things in the house."

"You listen to it at the store," said Gladys.

"That's different," said Sina.

"It's a slippery slope," said Old Tom, who had finally pushed away his burnt potatoes and begun eating corn-flakes with the rest of us. "From radios to flush toilets to electricity. Then before you know it, you're living life secondhand. You don't talk to people face-to-face any-more because the people on the radio are so much more interesting. And you don't play the piano and sing to-gether of an evening 'cause you've got the radio to do it for you. And then suddenly you start to think that unless you're sitting in that chair at six o'clock every night lis-tening to the radio, you're missing out on something. And someone starts to try to talk to you and you say, Shush, I'm listening to the radio. And soon you think you have to monitor all that stuff on the radio—the news, the music, the comedy shows, the talk shows. You think everyone else is monitoring it, too, and you know what? They are! They're listening to this object and not to each other. No one is living together anymore in communities and villages and with their kith and kin and friends and enemies. No, they're living in the vicinity of other people but not with them. They're living with the radio. But they feel like something's missing. And it is. Because the *radio* doesn't know they're there."

"Oh, bunk," said Gladys.

"It's not bunk, it's maybe a little overstated . . ." said Sina.

"Is not," said Old Tom.

"But," Sina interrupted him, rushing on, "I'll tell you what isn't bunk and that's those radio waves. I don't believe they can possibly be good for you. Why, some people who have gotten both electricity and radio have nothing but waves bombarding them, slicing through their mortal beings day and night. Banging around the inside of their house, maybe mangling their brain waves, interfering with things . . ."

"What things?" demanded Gladys.

"Well, we don't know, do we?" said Old Tom. "With a science so young? Maybe the next generation will be born with three eyes. How'd you like that? Having a three-eyed baby?" Old Tom crossed his arms as if this settled things, and he and Sina nodded to each other across the table.

"Right," said Gladys. "Well, it's your funeral. I shall do my best, but don't expect nothing in the future that ain't burnt or ruined in some way because my back brain never got given a chance."

"Don't say 'ain't' at my dinner table," said Sina grumpily. "Not in front of the children."

"You're not very nice employers," Gladys said. "You're not very nice people. And I like saying 'ain't.'"

"We're perfectly nice people," said Sina. "We just don't like radios. Or sloppy speech."

And then, although the weather had been fine all day, there was a terrific clap of thunder and the windows blackened and the wind roared in off the ocean. Old Tom and Sina got up and ran out to get all the animals inside their stalls.

Wilfred stood and said, "I'm going to see if Old Tom needs help," and ran outdoors, too. Then when Zebediah saw them running around like maniacs in the rain, he decided to run out and be an airplane among them and was flying through the mud, his arms extended, making buzzing sounds. Tag and Molly were galloping past him one way as Old Tom drove them into the barn, and the cows were driven by Sina another way and I watched in fascination, wondering if something terrible wasn't about to happen. It certainly looked chaotic, but the sense of foreboding could equally have been from the drop in barometric pressure, which always makes for a pleasantly ominous atmosphere.

Winifred leapt up and said, "This is my chance. I'm going to search for Daddy's letter!"

I could hear her taking the stairs two at a time up to Zebediah's room. I had just started to gather the dishes to take into the kitchen, where Gladys was already up to her elbows in soapsuds, when I felt a draft blowing through the dining room. I froze and put the dishes down again. At first I thought the draft came from the fireplace, but then I realized it was unlikely as we never used that fireplace and when I checked the flue it was tightly shut. Then I thought someone might have left the front door open, but when I looked into the front hall I could see that it was closed. There was an odd chill in the air. A dead chill, I thought in retrospect, but that was only after. I had never felt such a chill. As I stood there wondering what was causing it, the dining room curtains shut on their own. The window they covered was closed, the outside wind had not permeated inside, and anyhow, no wind could have caused two sides of the curtains to pull together. I didn't scream. As I found out, you don't when your brain simply cannot process quickly enough what it is seeing. And then, terrifyingly, I felt something like icy fingers on my shoulder and a second later I saw it—a white blur passed through the room. Suddenly I grasped the situation. It could be only one thing. And I ran to the front door yelling before my thoughts had even gelled, *"Ghost! Ghost!"*

In my hysteria, I became convinced that the ghost was keeping me prisoner. We have a sliding bolt lock, and I pushed and pushed the bolt to the open position to no avail. Why did the ghost not want me to leave? What did it plan to do with me? I continued screaming, *"Ghost! Ghost!"* and just as Gladys ran into the front hall, I realized the reason the bolt wouldn't slide any farther to the left was that it was already open and unlocked. I grabbed the doorknob, flung the door wide, and ran past Zebediah, still pretending to be an airplane, screaming, *"Ghost! Ghost! Ghost!"*

It was therefore something of a letdown to arrive inside the barn, where Sina was calmly filling the horses' buckets with grain, and Old Tom and Wilfred were busily forking hay down and paying no attention to me.

"Ghooooooooost!" I hollered for good measure, thinking perhaps that none of them had heard me. How else to explain their greeting this phenomenon so calmly? How little I remembered my own reaction to Sina screaming "UFO!"

Indeed, Sina turned to face me, all skepticism, and said, "Really, Franny. You say banana, I say banahna. Let's call the whole thing off."

"What?" I said, still thinking she must have heard wrong. Or, perhaps, finally indulged in a nervous breakdown from the strain of having houseguests.

"I see a UFO, so you have to see a ghost?"

"Are you saying it wasn't a ghost, that it was your UFO I saw?" I asked, still confused.

"No, I'm saying you are playing can-you-top-this. I'm surprised at you."

Then I got it. She thought I was trying to make myself important through the medium of ghosts. Suddenly I was less terrified than annoyed. "Are you saying I *didn't* see a ghost?" I demanded.

"I just thought you were a little more original. Ghosts

are very close to UFOs, phenomena-wise," said Sina, filling the horses' and cows' water buckets.

"Are not!" I said.

"What do you think, Tom?" asked Sina.

"I think Franny thought she saw a ghost and I think you thought you saw a UFO and I think you've all got the jimjams. You're nutters, every one of you. Except Wilfred," said Old Tom, patting him affectionately on the shoulder as they threw more hay down from the loft. Old Tom had clearly taken a shine to Wilfred after working side by side with him most of the day, and I was suddenly filled with a jealousy so violent that it was all I could do to keep from pushing Wilfred into a pile of manure. Let's see if that will disturb his phlegmatic calm, I thought temptingly, but, of course, reined myself in in time.

"Nobody likes a copycat," said Sina.

"Well, excuse me," I said. "But if we could believe you about the UFO, you might at least entertain the notion of a ghost."

"You *didn't* believe me!" protested Sina. "You did nothing but joke about it."

"Be fair," I said. "Only Old Tom joked about it."

"Yes, but the rest of you obviously thought I was cracked."

I said nothing. This much was true. It was clear that we were all now less interested in whether these phenomena were real than we were in using them to beat each other over the head for still extant grudges.

We finished watering and feeding the animals in a sullen silence, and then Sina and I took off through the pounding rain to the house. Wilfred ran to grab a buzzing Zebediah and drag him inside, and Old Tom went to make sure all the outbuildings were closed up. Inside, Winifred could be heard scurrying around upstairs. When she came down she had a suspiciously innocent look on her face.

"Did you find it?" I whispered.

"No, dagnabbit," she whispered back. "Maybe you can distract Zebediah later and I can sneak up again. I can see it isn't in his pants pocket, which was where it was when he came home, so I am sure it is no longer on him but must be hidden somewhere in his room. I checked all his drawers and bedding, but he's a master hider. I need more time."

Sina and I went into the kitchen to help Gladys finish up while the others came in to watch and drip on the kitchen floor. I began to elaborate on what I had seen. I was pleased to note that when Sina got the long version, she began to show a little concern. It seemed to be finally sinking in that I hadn't made up the ghost simply to top her UFO. But Gladys just shrugged.

"Oh yeah, ghosts," she said, as if ghosts were a dime a dozen where she came from. "I heard you yell 'Ghost,' but it must have cheesed it by the time I got there. Well, there's only one way to get rid of ghosts, and that's to smudge."

"I've heard it said cinnamon is effective," said Sina vaguely. Sina had all kinds of bits and pieces of information crashing around her brain from her long and varied life on earth. Apparently now that she'd decided there *was* a ghost, she was prepared to retrieve something useful from her store.

"Well," said Gladys, "cinnamon is all right, but if you ask me there's nothing like a good smudging. If you get me some sage and rosemary from the garden, I'll show you how. Then that ghost won't bother you anymore."

"It's pouring rain," said Sina. "We'll have nothing but puddles all over the floor if people keep going out."

"Do you want puddles or ghosts?" asked Gladys.

Sina turned on her heel at this and was going out the

front door to get sage and rosemary when Old Tom came in, shaking himself like a big wet dog.

"Where are you going?" he asked.

"To get rosemary and sage. To burn. Smudging. It drives away the ghosts."

"Starved for entertainment," said Old Tom.

"You can help if you like," said Sina.

"I believe I will give this one a pass," said Old Tom and went upstairs to read.

Once we had the herbs, Gladys dried them because they were soaking wet from the rain, tied them tightly, and then lit them. All of us but Old Tom walked solemnly about the dining room in parade formation behind Gladys, who was either speaking a lot of drivel she was making up on the spot (which is what I primarily believed) or incanting just the right ghost-exterminating words. It smelled nice anyway, the smoke, sort of like Thanksgiving.

"Maybe the ghost has moved to another room," said Zebediah. "Maybe we should smudge all the rooms."

"There's no such thing," said Wilfred. "I'm going up to read."

Well, who's become Old Tom's little acolyte? I thought sourly.

"I am, too," said Zebediah. "This is creepy."

"No, you aren't," said Winifred.

"Yes, I am," said Zebediah.

"You must stay, mustn't he, Franny?" said Winifred. "Because I have always heard tell that a little boy must be part of the smudging. For full potency."

"Hogwash," said Gladys. "I never heard anything so silly."

"Oh, look who's talking silly," said Winifred. "Stay ten minutes, Zebediah, and I'll read you a chapter of *The Young Man's Flight Manual*."

"Two chapters," said Zebediah.

"One," said Winifred.

"One and a half."

"All right. Now I have to go take my bath. You stay and smudge."

"I don't want to be here all alone," said Zebediah.

"You aren't, you little twit. You have Franny and Sina and Gladys."

"I mean the only one of our family smudging."

"Don't be rude. You're *representing* the family," said Winifred. "It's a great honor." And she hightailed it upstairs to search for the letter again.

We did one more circuit around the dining room

table, but I could tell that Gladys was running out of speed.

"Well, that's that," said Sina. "If there *was* a ghost, he's had a good smudging now. Let's sprinkle a little cinnamon around and call it a night."

"NO!" I cried, wanting to buy more time for Winifred, and then was startled when Gladys cried "NO!" too.

"I am getting vibrations!" she said.

"Ghostly vibrations?" I asked, goose bumps coming out all over my arms. Despite the current fun and games, it really had been the most chilling experience.

"No. Psychic vibrations, and they're coming from . . ." Gladys spun in a circle looking at each of us in turn, her eyes all scrunched up as if in deep concentration or communing with the beyond. "From YOU!" She pointed at Sina suddenly. Sina gave a little yip and shuffled back a foot.

"Yes, you are emanating particularly strongly right now," Gladys said, nodding. "It's an excellent time to do a reading."

"A reading of what?" asked Sina, taking the burning herbs out of Gladys's hand and putting them in the fireplace before we accidentally burned the house down.

"Your emanations," said Gladys.

"What is this going to cost me?" asked Sina, looking at Gladys skeptically.

"I'm hurt, I truly am," said Gladys, pulling up a dining room chair and sitting down. "Do you think I would charge my own dear employer for a spiritual service?"

"Well, I *would* think so, yes," said Sina. "But if you say it's free, then why not?"

Zebediah and I pulled up chairs, too. This was less creepy but more thrilling than the smudging.

"Now," said Gladys, "give me your hands."

"Do I have to?" asked Sina.

"Don't you know *anything*?" asked Gladys, forgetting to be charming and just being her old snotty self.

"Well, yes, I think I know *some* things. You must forgive me if I'm not up on the latest hoodoo-voodoo," said Sina, who could give as good as she got.

"Hands!" snapped Gladys.

So Sina put her hands in Gladys's.

The atmosphere was, as they say, charged. Between the smoke, which still hung in the air, the wind roaring through the pine trees, the sound of the surf crashing, the dark house—we had yet to light the coal lanterns and were still burning the dinner candles—and our own taut, creeped-out faces, it was quite the dramatic setting.

In such an environ do ghosts appear. I was keeping a sharp eye out.

"State your full name," said Gladys in sepulchral tones.

"Do I have to?" asked Sina.

"Name!" snapped Gladys. This constant leapfrogging from psychic mystery woman to snot bucket was very disorienting.

I could see it was throwing Sina off balance because she spat out "Thomasina Maria Whitekraft" obediently.

"Thomasina Maria, I have three things to tell you. First, your gift and it *is* a gift is that you have no idea how beautiful you are. Remember, this is a gift. Your great shining beauty and your unawarity."

"I don't think 'unawarity' is a word," I said.

"Hush," said Sina. "I think she may know what she's doing after all. Go on."

"Second, you have great talent. You are likewise unaware of this."

I noticed she didn't use "unawarity" again and counted this a victory.

Sina, although I'm sure she tried not to, preened.

"Third, UFOs will be trying to contact you via the radio. This is most important, *most important . . .*" And then Gladys scared the bejesus out of us by fluttering her eyelids and fainting, sliding off her chair and falling right to the floor.

Sina leapt up, but at the same time Winifred could be heard crashing down the stairs, taking them, as was her wont, two at a time.

"I *found* it! I *found* it! And what the blue blazes does this mean, you little snake?" she cried, bursting into the dining room and holding up over her head, for all to see, a piece of paper with four words written in block letters: NOW IS THE TIME.

SECRETS

ive that to me!" shouted Zebediah, standing on his chair in an attempt to reach the paper and lunging for it.

This caused his chair to tip over and fall on Gladys, who hollered, "OW! Did you not just see me fall into a deadly swoon from the strength of the emanations? Have a little respect!"

"Stop that right now and get up," said Sina. "It's time we all went to bed."

Gladys started to get up, but Winifred and Zebediah, who were fighting tooth and claw above her in a way I had never before seen, a no-holds-barred, fingernail-digging and hair-pulling free-for-all, suddenly fell directly on top of her. Gladys screamed bloody murder as you'd expect, but oddly this didn't penetrate either

Zebediah's or Winifred's rage—they continued pummeling each other directly on top of her, creating so much noise that Old Tom came running downstairs, followed by Wilfred, and between the two of them they managed to separate Zebediah and Winifred, who, although they were pinioned, continued to lash out at each other while Gladys shouted, "What about *me*?"

"You? Go to bed, you," said Sina, sitting down wearily and beginning to light the coal lanterns.

"What, you mean to my cabin? I'm not going out there in the dark all alone. There are *ghosts*!" Gladys reminded her.

"Ghosts? I wouldn't be worried about the ghosts if I were you," said Old Tom. "I'd be worried about the cougars. But to each his own. And, you two, why can't you be more like your brother? Wilfred is a model of ideal deportment. You'd never catch him—"

But he was cut off by Wilfred, who had just seen the letter from their father with the mysterious NOW IS THE TIME and erupted with "Were you keeping this a secret, you little wretch?" and promptly bopped Zebediah on the head.

Obviously, given Wilfred's cool and collected nature, this was a surprise to all of us. It did not seem to be a surprise to Zebediah, who was apparently used to such treatment.

"Oh, for God's sake, go to bed, the three of you," said Old Tom, not caring that Wilfred had bopped Zebediah but annoyed that he had done it in the middle of what was to be a stirring speech exhorting Wilfred's virtues.

"Go to bed, everyone," said Sina.

"I'm not going out there with the ghosts!" shouted Gladys.

So Old Tom very kindly picked up a coal lantern, lit it, and proceeded to escort her across the yard to her cabin. You could hear them over the wind and the rain yelling.

"There's no such thing!"

"Yes there is!"

"No there's not!"

"IS!"

"There's cougars. There's bears. There's owls that might fly at you and scratch your eyes out. There's bats. There's wolves. There's enough things to be afraid of out here. But there *ARE NO GHOSTS!*"

"Are!" said Gladys.

After Old Tom left with Gladys, Sina turned to us with fierce eyes and said, "Go to bed, each and every one of you, and no speaking. I don't dare let anyone in this house interact any more tonight, for it's clear there's a friction in the air that will ignite with the least provocation. We must not make contact with each other."

Then, as we all stood staring dumbly at her, trying to ingest this loquacious tidbit, she narrowed her eyes and barked "GO!" in a most un-Sina-like way and we scattered off to our rooms like so many rabbits making for so many holes. The Madden children went up to their bedrooms, but I went up to the cupola to write about the ghost.

Although I felt full of the magic and mystery of this and wrote fiendishly, when I reread what I'd written there was, as usual, something missing. I should have known better than to try to make a story out of an actual event. I tried to insert a mermaid, but that was no help. I wasn't an idiot; I knew you couldn't make stories by just sticking things together and hoping for the best, that wherever stories came from, it wasn't from your own clever little mind, but even so, I sighed, one must try. So I tried again, but that didn't work either. I was beginning to think that when there is magic in a story it isn't because something magical is being written about. The story itself seems to be magic. And I couldn't help feeling that had nothing to do with its author. I wanted to will this magic into my stories yet had been unable to do so. It was very frustrating. Many people write good enough stories, but few write ones that are magic. Finally I just went to bed.

I lay awake for a while listening for disturbances, but the only disturbance was Sina knocking on my door and coming in to say she had something to tell me. And when she was done my head was spinning, but at least after that it was a quiet night.

+ ✦ +

Sunday dawned clear and calm. Most of us were in our right minds again or at least keeping up a modest pretext of it. When we appeared for breakfast we found nothing prepared and no sign of Gladys. Sina went worriedly to her cabin, saying she hoped Gladys wasn't ill, but I could tell that after all the hoopla of the past few days she thought anything might have happened to her—ghosts, UFOs—as far as uninvited guests went, we at East Sooke Farm had it all.

When Sina returned, she looked utterly bewildered.

She sat down at the kitchen table next to us children, who were wondering if breakfast would be prepared or if we should make our own. At first Sina said nothing, just stared ahead as if puzzling something out, and then turned to us and said, "Gladys will not be cooking today."

"Oh dear," I said. "Men from Mars?"

"She says it's her day off. She says it is union-mandated."

"Is she a member of a cooking union?" asked Winifred in surprise.

"So she says," said Sina. "And she accused me of trying to run a sweatshop. I said that I thought you needed a lot of people to run a sweatshop and she said no, you needed only sweat."

When Old Tom came in from feeding the animals and saw there was no breakfast, he puttered around making coffee and pancakes for everyone. On learning why Gladys hadn't cooked, he looked rather happy and said, "Never mind, I'll make my roast chicken. Best chicken you've ever had, children. And I see you've already picked one out, Franny."

"Yes," I said.

"Bad layer?" he asked.

"Bad all-around chicken," I said, and looked the other way. I preferred Old Tom not to get wind of my chicken-culling methods, so I changed the subject. "Sina, would you make paper dolls for Winifred and me?" Sina made the best paper dolls in the world. She could give them any nuance of expression you wanted. Winifred and I were rather old to *play* with paper dolls but not too old to *own* them.

"Certainly," said Sina, and the three of us began to plan a whole family of very snooty dolls. Wilfred and Old Tom sat at the opposite end of the dining room table, where we'd moved to eat breakfast, planning their work for the day, and so we hardly noticed when Zebediah slipped out, made for the woods, and didn't return until lunch.

✦ ✦ ✦

"Boys," said Sina after lunch when she saw Zebediah race out the door again, "need lots of time and leeway to explore and get into trouble. It helps them get it out of their systems before they become men." Then she drew a series of paper-doll boys hanging by their ankles from trees and falling off cliffs and such. We thought it was very funny at the time because we had no idea what Zebediah was actually up to.

And all in all the day passed peacefully, culminating in the most delightful of roast chicken meals. Gladys deigned to join us and lifted not a finger to help in either the preparation or cleanup, but we ignored this, which I think she found a little disappointing.

✦ ✦ ✦

Monday morning, Zebediah took off for the woods again.

Winifred and I had just started to gather eggs when Wilfred came by the chicken coop with a wheelbarrow.

"I need to get some compost," he said. "Old Tom said that because we have the potato field and kitchen garden under control, we can take a morning to do a quick compost blitz of the other gardens. I'm taking wheelbarrow loads to all of them."

"I love the flower gardens," said Winifred, turning to me as we watched Wilfred shovel compost from the pile a little way from the chicken coop. "Do you have a favorite? I like the one with the really tall flowers."

"That's the English garden," I said. "It's my favorite, too. It has hollyhocks and Canterbury bells and lupines and poppies. We don't know who planted it. We think it might have been Old Tom's aunt Bertha, but we're not sure. When I was little I used to play there all the time because it looked like just the sort of garden where fairies would live. Sina's favorite is the Italian garden."

Winifred and I grabbed shovels and walked over to help Wilfred. As the three of us took a wheelbarrowful across one of the many hayfields to the English garden, I pointed to the formal boxwood maze and hedge patterns of the Italian garden in the corner of the farm. Next to it was the statuary garden, which required little care, being mostly dwarf trees and statues.

"The Italian garden, the statuary garden, and the herb garden were planted by the people who put in tennis courts and had fabulous parties," I said. "Old Tom never liked those gardens much because they have no flowers and the boxwood needs constant pruning. He would have bulldozed them except for Sina. He doesn't see the beauty in the Italian garden the way she does. The herb garden also has boxwood that needs pruning, but it's low to the ground and planted to separate the different herbs into geometric beds. Old Tom says the tennis-court people must have loved boxwood. He doesn't mind trimming it in the herb garden so much because at least you get herbs out of it and the boxwood has a useful purpose there."

"He says we're not doing anything in the wildflower garden or the garden of exotic blooms today," said Wilfred as we dumped compost in the English garden and went to get the next load for the heliotrope garden.

"The heliotrope garden is my second favorite," I said as we filled the wheelbarrow again, "because it's so romantic and smells so good. Mrs. Brown put it in. But it needs constant pinching back. I try to go in whenever I pass it and pinch it back a bit each time, because I'm afraid that if one garden were to be plowed under it would be that one. Old Tom wants to expand the vegetable growing, but it means losing one of the flower gardens. He'll never plow under the Japanese garden, because that's his favorite even though he always says he's sorry he ever put it in."

"I guess people aren't very nice about it since the war," said Wilfred knowledgeably.

"Oh no, Old Tom doesn't care about that," I said. "No, he says it's because taking care of it is such a bear. But I know he doesn't mean it. It's the one he truly loves, and he fusses over it the most with all its precise plantings and little walkways. It's also the one he's spent the most money on. Every time he does something new in it, it reveals something else that should be there. First it was stone lanterns that led to a little bridge over the creek. After that he dammed the creek and made a water lily pond. The lily pond revealed a need for a pergola with wisteria hanging from it in long lavender strands. Which revealed a lack of koi, so he started buying koi, which the herons ate until he figured out a netting he could put over the top of the pond to keep them out. Whenever a true gardener visits the farm it's the Japanese garden they ooh and aah over."

We worked in silence for a bit after that. The last load we dumped was in the Japanese garden. Winifred and I stopped to sniff the wisteria. I didn't spend a lot of time in the Japanese garden. It was a little persnickety for my taste, but the wisteria smelled wonderful. If Old Tom ever needed some peace, he could be found on the stone bench by the tiny waterfall he had built. He said there was nothing like listening to the sound of water burbling to calm yourself.

Then Old Tom called from the English garden, and

Wilfred trotted off there to help weed and to spread the compost.

Winifred and I headed back to the chicken coop to finish gathering, candling, and packing eggs.

"Aren't we supposed to leave compost outside the night garden?" asked Winifred as we packed the last egg and picked the boxes up to take to the root cellar to keep cool.

Before I could answer, Sina came into the egg-candling room and broke all precedent by saying, "Franny, dear, can you put the eggs and milk into the truck? I'm going to Brookman's."

"But you were just there Saturday," I said.

"Yes, I know, but I can go again if I like, I guess. And besides, Zebediah wants me to mail his letter for him."

"Zebediah is writing to Mother and Daddy?" asked Winifred.

Sina pulled the letter out of her pocket and said, "No, just your father apparently."

Winifred and I looked at each other.

"What?" said Sina. "Why shouldn't he write to his father?"

"No reason," said Winifred and I together.

Sina gave us a long, speculative look, so I said, "Anyhow, Sina, you never go to Brookman's more than once a week. You always say that to go more often would cost us in gas what little profit we make on the eggs and milk."

"I know what I say, Franny. Nonetheless."

"Can we go, too?" asked Winifred.

"Well," said Sina, clearly not happy about the idea, "I suppose I can't stop you."

I couldn't imagine why Sina wouldn't want Winifred and me to go. We were charming company. So we put the eggs and milk in the truck and ran inside to get any muck we had accumulated off us and to put on clean shirts.

＊✦＊

At Brookman's everyone was drinking coffee. Sina gave us each a nickel again, and I wondered if she'd forgotten she'd done so on Saturday because a nickel was usually a once-a-week occurrence at best. Winifred and I decided to get the candy that was easiest to split among the four of us, as we didn't feel that it was fair to shut Wilfred and Zebediah out of any unusual nickel bonanzas that came our way. We were poised between the Smarties and the Sugar Babies when I noticed that Sina was behaving in a most peculiar way. She stood seemingly among the gossiping women but still slightly outside their tight little circle and a bit closer to the counter where the radio sat. And then while I watched, her hand surreptitiously slid across the counter and gave the volume control just the slightest tweak. I stopped choosing candy and kept my eye on her after that, and sure enough a few minutes later her hand made the journey to the volume dial again. She was standing in a strange position, her eyes turned expectantly to the women, and she seemed to nod when they did and laugh when they did, but from her expression I didn't think she was hearing a thing that was being said.

"What about bubble gum?" asked Winifred in a loud voice. "Instead of Sugar Babies?"

"*Shh!*" said Sina in a louder voice that caused everyone to stop talking.

"I . . . I didn't mean you," Sina said to the ladies. Everyone continued to look at her inquisitively. "I didn't mean you either," she said to Winifred. "Or you," she said to me.

"Who did you mean then, dear?" asked Mrs. Brookman.

"I meant, um, I meant the man on the radio. He has one of those annoying voices," said Sina. Then she blushed.

"He can't hear you," said Miss Macy. "I know because I have also tried to converse with those smart and interesting radio men. Sometimes it gets so lonely. In the house. By myself. The radio men seem like such pleasant fellows. But I've come to the conclusion that they can't hear me. No matter how loudly I speak."

"Which radio men, dear?" asked Mrs. Brookman.

"All of them," said Miss Macy.

The ladies quietly rolled their eyes, Winifred and I bought our candy, and the conversation picked up again so Sina, Winifred, and I slunk out and went back home to have lunch.

After lunch Winifred and I dutifully split the candy into four piles, but it was very unsatisfactory, as Wilfred, instead of exclaiming at our sense of fair play and his delight at having been unexpectedly gifted with confectionary largesse, just put his candy in his pocket and went back outside to help Old Tom.

Winifred put her hand over Zebediah's pile and said, "This candy is for you, but only if you tell me about this big secret you and Daddy share."

Zebediah said, "Never."

So he got no candy at all. It was more for Winifred and me, but that was hardly the point.

This worried Winifred. "If he is choosing this secret over candy, it must be very serious. Wilfred isn't worried about Zebediah's secret little correspondence with Daddy; he is just annoyed at Zebediah because we had all agreed some time ago to pool information about Mother and Daddy and their doings. But now I think Wilfred *should* be worried. We should all be worried."

+ ✦ +

Tuesday passed normally, but Wednesday Sina decided to go to Brookman's again. Zebediah was off by himself, and Wilfred was with Old Tom, so once again it was only Winifred and I who tagged along. Afterward, when Sina settled herself in the truck and looked through the mail, she said, "Another letter for Zebediah."

Winifred and I shot each other looks but said nothing.

"I don't like this," Winifred whispered to me once we got home. "We need to get a hold of that letter."

"Sina," I said, "why don't Winifred and I find Zebediah and give him his letter?"

"No need," said Sina. "'I'll give it to him at dinner."

She took it into the studio with her own mail and held it until dinnertime, when she presented it to Zebediah, back from his day in the woods, so there was no chance to steal it.

+ ✦ +

Thursday, Zebediah gave Sina another letter for Mr. Madden, which Sina promised dutifully to mail that day at Brookman's. Then Zebediah took off for the woods.

"This is terrible," said Winifred to me as we loaded what milk and eggs we had accumulated into the truck. "She shouldn't feel obligated to take time out of her busy day to be his personal postman."

"I don't think that's entirely why she's going," I said. "You've seen her around the radio. It is very strange. I think there's something she's not telling us. It's not like her to be so secretive. It's certainly not like her to be running back and forth to Brookman's so often."

"*Everyone* is suddenly so secretive," said Winifred. "Daddy, Zebediah, Sina. You don't suppose they're in on something together?"

"Whatever could your father and Zebediah and Sina

be in on together? And where is your mother in all this? Or Old Tom? No, I think Wilfred may be right, the letters may be quite innocent. After all, Zebediah can barely print, right? He's probably just sending your father pictures of planes he's drawn or something and trying to make himself important."

"What about the one from Daddy that said 'NOW IS THE TIME'?" asked Winifred.

"Who knows? Time to keep fit. Time to learn how to print better. I don't know. I wouldn't worry about it."

"Too late for that," said Winifred.

Family Meeting

ut on Saturday, Winifred caught a break when on our return from Brookman's Sina pulled a letter for Zebediah from the stack and handed it to her saying, "I think I saw Zebediah heading back from the woods. Do you want to run and give him this?"

Winifred grabbed it wildly before Sina could change her mind. Sina went back to sorting through and reading her own mail and didn't notice when we ran up to my bedroom, where Winifred opened it. It was from Fixing Bob and, like the first note, was in block letters: KEEP IT TO YOURSELF BUT FIND OUT MORE.

"Oh dear, oh dear. Wilfred will have to be concerned now," Winifred said. "We must show it to him and we must present a united front against Zebediah. I don't like the sound of this. This must have something to do with why Mother went up to Comox to the air force base. Maybe this time Daddy really is doing something stupid!"

"But what stupid thing can your father be planning? And why tell Zebediah?" I asked.

"I don't know," said Winifred worriedly. "But we will find out. Believe me."

Winifred pulled Wilfred aside right before we went into lunch and showed him the letter. They decided to hold a meeting with Zebediah to get to the bottom of things. I was pleased to be included in what, after all, might be considered a family matter.

There was no talking at lunch. Perhaps because Gladys had put maraschino cherries in the tuna fish salad and we were all, even Gladys, focused on finding them with our tongues and spitting them into napkins without anyone else seeing. *Do not waste food. Children in Europe are starving!* was ingrained on all our brains both from posters everywhere and from the grown-ups chanting it. Never chanting it when we were eating candy, of course, only when we wouldn't eat objectionable foods like spinach. Despite everyone's feelings for the poor starving children in Europe, it was clear we were bent on wasting the maraschinos, so we shouldn't have bothered pretending not to. All, that is, except Zebe-diah, who kept saying "Yum yum yum" every time he hit a cherry and so was, I fear, encouraging Gladys in her culinary flights of fancy. Or perhaps we were all just deep in thought. I couldn't tell. There was no dessert. Apparently the tuna-maraschino confection was a one-dish wonder incorporating salad, sandwich, and dessert.

After lunch, without telling Zebediah anything except that a family meeting was happening, we headed to the beach.

When we got there the tide was high, so we sat on big boulders and stared silently out to sea as we tried to figure out how to broach the sticky subject of the letters.

"All right, then, I call this meeting to order," said Wilfred finally. "Zebediah, you may suspect why we are having it."

"No," said Zebediah.

"No, you don't suspect why?" said Winifred.

"No, I won't tell you," said Zebediah. "You want to know what Daddy meant by 'NOW IS THE TIME.' And I won't tell you because I promised not to tell anyone."

"Actually," said Winifred, whipping the new letter, which she had kept from him, out of her pocket, "we have his latest letter to you and we want to know what he means by 'KEEP IT TO YOURSELF BUT FIND OUT MORE.'"

"That's my letter!" said Zebediah, jumping up to grab it.

But Winifred was too fast for him. Wilfred leapt up, grabbed Zebediah, and sat on him. Winifred put the letter back in her pocket.

"If Daddy said keep it to yourself, he didn't mean to keep it from us," said Wilfred, panting from the exertion of keeping Zebediah under him. "Why would Daddy write to you and not us?"

"Because I write to him," said Zebediah. "And I know things you don't."

"You do not," said Winifred.

"I do, too," said Zebediah.

"Oh, really? Then what is Daddy telling you it is time for?" said Wilfred. "I'll tell you what he thought it was time for; he thought it was time for you to tell us what is going on."

"You don't know anything," said Zebediah.

"That's the point," said Wilfred. "So tell us. And remember, we promised a long time ago to share any information about Mother and Daddy between the three of us. It's very important that we children have a united front."

"I promised Daddy, and I'm keeping my promise," said Zebediah. "The last time he came home he told me something he didn't tell you. He said it was our little secret."

"You snake," said Winifred. "You're *especially* supposed to share Mother and Daddy's secrets!"

"Zebediah," said Wilfred, "sharing is essential."

"Yes," said Winifred. "Didn't Franny and I share our candy with you when we might have kept it secretly for ourselves?"

"No, you didn't. You said I could have it only if I told you my secret," said Zebediah, outraged.

"Precisely," said Winifred. "You didn't get candy because you didn't share. You have to learn to share, Zebediah. It's a *sin* not to share. If you don't share this, Wilfred and I won't share anything else with you. Not our candy, not our secrets, nothing. And when you die, you'll go to hell. With ghosts and goblins."

"I do share!" cried Zebediah. "Even if I don't share what I'm not supposed to, I do share. I share all kinds of things."

"No you don't, you little sneak," said Winifred. "You run off to the woods every day and don't tell us what you do all day long. You get letters from Daddy that I'm sure he would want you to share, and you don't."

"You never asked me what I do in the woods," yelled Zebediah, looking frantic. "And I'm not going to hell with ghosts and goblins."

"Not willingly," said Winifred.

"You get dragged there," said Wilfred, looking studiously unconcerned.

"By your hair," said Winifred.

I thought the ghosts-and-goblins-in-hell bit was laying it on a little thick, but it wasn't my family. Clearly this was a tried-and-true method of getting Zebediah to spill the beans.

"You're not even going to the hell with ghosts and goblins; you're going to an especially bad hell for little boys who keep secrets from their siblings," said Winifred, "someplace where there are such terrible beings we've never even heard of them. But I'll tell you this, Zebediah Madden: they make ghosts and goblins look cuddly."

"Now, now, let's be reasonable, Winifred," said Wilfred,

laying a calming hand on her forearm and then turning to Zebediah. "Let's give him a chance to tell us. Zebediah, what *do* you do in the woods all day?"

"I visit the hermit," said Zebediah.

"No you don't," I said. I couldn't help myself. "You can't make us believe he made friends with you just because he caught you spying on him. The hermit doesn't want to spend time with anyone. That's why he's a hermit."

"Ipso facto," said Wilfred.

I didn't know what "ipso facto" meant but made a note to look it up. Bonus points, Wilfred!

"He wants to spend time with *me*," said Zebediah. "He likes me. He showed me where the mermaid rescued him from the ocean."

"Oh, please," said Winifred. "Mermaids!"

"She did, she did."

"Liar," said Winifred.

"I'm *not*," said Zebediah. "That's what the hermit told me, and he even showed me some of the scales that fell off her. They're made of gold, and he keeps them in a special box."

"Oh, you big fat liar," said Winifred. "It's one thing not to tell us stuff, but to make up such rubbish!"

"I didn't! He did!" said Zebediah. He had given up struggling under Wilfred, but he could still shout.

"All right, let's go ask him," said Wilfred.

"He won't tell you. He doesn't like people," said Zebediah. "He told me so. But he likes *me*. He likes *me* because I'm special."

"You are not," said Winifred. "I never heard of such a thing."

"And even if it *is* true," said Wilfred, "you stay away from him. He's a crazy person. Mother wouldn't want you going off visiting a crazy person like that all on your own."

"Oh, he's harmless," I said. "Really. Old Tom would never let him stay here if he wasn't."

"What about Daddy?" shrieked Winifred, turning to Zebediah.

"I'll never tell you, and you can't make me!" screamed Zebediah back.

There was a moment's peace as we all sat silently, not knowing where to take things from here.

It was Zebediah who spoke first, this time in calm tones. "All right. Maybe I should have told you. If you get off me and let me read my letter, I will tell you what it all means."

Wilfred looked at Winifred. She shrugged and took Zebediah's letter out of her pocket.

"Promise?" she asked.

Zebediah nodded solemnly as best he could from his prone position, and Wilfred got off him. But before anyone could move, Zebediah leapt up, grabbed the letter out of Winifred's hand, and made for the woods.

"Liar, liar, pants on fire! We'll never trust you again, Zebediah! I hope you're happy now!" screamed Winifred.

As we leapt up, prepared to race after Zebediah, Old Tom approached, calling to Wilfred that it was time to work in the garden, and we lost our chance.

"I gotta go," said Wilfred. And he was gone, too.

"Mermaids, UFOs, ghosts," said Winifred. "Honestly."

"Yes, honestly, have you ever heard such nonsense?" I said. And then added quietly, "Except for the ghost."

"Let's go ask your mother about the letters," said Winifred. "Maybe, just maybe, Zebediah has told her something."

So we trooped up to the studio, where Sina was circling a half-formed clay mermaid as if she were a boxer looking for an opening. When we came in we startled her and she said, "Oh, dadblast it! I think I almost almost had it. Now it's gone."

"Oh, Sina, I'm sorry," I said.

"We'll go, Mrs. Whitekraft," said Winifred. "We'll leave immediately to let your genius percolate again."

"Genius, feh," said Sina, knocking the clay to the ground. "Never mind, it was never going to come to me, it's all a tease really. What did you want?"

"Has Zebediah told you anything about the letters he and his father are exchanging?" I asked.

"No," said Sina, looking surprised. "Why should he?"

"Right, that's fine. We were just checking," said Winifred.

"I must say, he has lovely printing for someone so young," Sina said distractedly, picking the lump of clay back up and throwing it on her pedestal to start again. And then she seemed a second later to forget we were there, so we crept out.

"Lovely printing!" said Winifred, incensed. "Zebediah's printing is way messier than mine was at that age."

"Never mind," I said. "Grown-ups are always speaking hyperbolically when it comes to children. Sina is always saying that I'm a stunning beauty, which even I, in my most wishful-thinking moments, know is utter bunk."

Winifred nodded, but I could tell her mind was elsewhere.

+ ✦ +

The rest of the day passed uneventfully. We turned in early to our separate quarters, having had really rather enough of each other. It was one thing having house-guests, and it was another having ones with their family dynamics thrown in. It was interesting but wearing.

I went up to my cupola because as engrossing as it had been watching Winifred and Wilfred interrogate Zebediah, I had begun to have new feelings for my mermaid story. I could sense it churning, a little ball of energy in the pit of my stomach, and I couldn't wait for my typewriter; my fingers were fairly itching for it. Perhaps something about Zebediah mentioning the hermit's mermaid had sparked it. Even before I knew about the hermit's mermaid or before Sina and I knew about each other's current projects, Sina had been working on her mermaid sculpture and I on my mermaid story. Mermaids seemed to be everywhere. It's as though these things are just in the air and people all grasp onto them at the same time. One year all the books are about dragons without any communication about this, the way one year everyone plants hollyhocks. They're just in front of everyone's house, but if asked people will say they don't know why they planted them; they just got the urge. Sina often said that, like it or not, we're all drinking from the same pond.

Finally, having written two pages I, too, went to bed.

✦

I think we were all hoping for a good night's sleep, but we were to be denied this because all of a sudden in the middle of the night we were awoken by a shout. And not just any shout but Old Tom's, and Old Tom was not given to shouting. I leapt up and ran to my window to see what the ruckus was all about.

There was a full moon and the night garden was wildly aglow. Only white flowers had been planted in the night garden in order to reflect the moonlight. The moonflowers open at dusk and close at dawn, their white trumpet-shaped blooms incandescent, like strings of lanterns all over the garden. There were white hydrangeas, white foxglove, and flowers like night-scented stock that released their scent only at night. If the breeze is right and I open my window and am awake to appreciate it, the smell of the night-blooming flowers wafts into my room mixed with the scent of the ocean. There are ancient old marble garden statues in the night garden, cherubim and griffins and phoenixes. Placed throughout are birdbaths of gleaming alabaster and solar stars and moon spinners whose globes at top, having absorbed the sun's rays all day, glow all night, their copper arms spinning with the night breezes. I always try to remember to get up the nights of the full moon to see the night garden in its glory, but I always frankly forget. I'm a sound sleeper. But not that night.

By moonlight I could make out Old Tom standing outside the night garden fence, waving his arms and shouting. Inside were two figures bent over. When they straightened up I could see they were the hermit and Zebediah. I opened my window and could hear Old Tom saying, "Get that boy out of there. What are you thinking? Any minute now he might wish. He might wish for anything. Good God, there's no telling what dangerous thing a boy will wish for."

140

The hermit said nothing but hoisted Zebediah up and all but threw him over the fence the way you might throw a pulled weed onto a compost heap and then went back to weeding the night garden as if nothing had happened. As if he were under the garden's spell.

"Don't let me ever—do you hear me?—*ever* find you in there again!" shouted Old Tom at Zebediah.

Poor Zebediah broke into tears with all this shouting and ran into the house, and I could hear Old Tom muttering to himself, "Good. Well, good. Had to be done."

The next thing I knew, Winifred and Wilfred, who it turned out had been watching from their rooms, were in my room and then a tearful Zebediah was heard running up the stairs. Wilfred ran into the hall, grabbed him, and dragged him back to my room. And then, despite my many misgivings, I had to tell them. After all, I thought, they had heard about UFOs, ghosts, and mermaids. They might as well hear about this, too.

THE NIGHT GARDEN

hat in the world?" said Winifred, sitting down on my bed. "Zebediah, what were you doing *in* the night garden?"

"I wanted to see the hermit," said Zebediah. "He told me that he would be weeding all night because it would be a full moon. I wanted to help him the way Wilfred helps Old Tom."

"Oh, for heaven's sake," said Winifred. "Listen, Zebediah, did you have to go *into* the garden, the one place Old Tom told you not to go?"

"I figured that if the hermit was in there, it had to be okay," said Zebediah, sniffling.

"Well, it's not," I said.

"I didn't know Old Tom would get so mad and *yell*," said Zebediah. "I thought everyone was asleep."

"Why *did* he get so mad?" whispered Wilfred, turning to me.

Old Tom hadn't yet come upstairs, but we didn't want to be heard banding together and talking about him if he did.

"Old Tom got so mad," I began, "because the night garden was planted magically a long time ago, so long ago that nobody really knows how long it has been here. Old Tom said that it may have been here since the dawn of time."

"What? Do you mean cavemen planted it?" asked Zebediah.

"No, before that. And family lore says that if you wish for something in the night garden, the wish will come true. But you only get one wish. And that wish can't be undone."

"Old Tom believes this? This wishing stuff?" asked Wilfred, looking skeptical.

"He believes it with every fiber of his being," I said. "He has the hermit working in the garden because Old Tom hasn't used his one wish yet. He says he's waiting for something spectacular and life-changing to wish for and so far it hasn't come along, but he says he will know it when it does. He is terrified of going into the night garden and thinking accidentally 'Hmmm, I wish we were having soup for lunch' or something and blowing the whole thing. He also says in the past people have wished for things that seemed innocent but turned out terribly for the wisher or innocent parties. He thinks children should not be allowed to wish in case they do damage to themselves and others and maybe the whole world; who knows what happens when wishes can be granted so easily and not undone afterward? And Sina has always said she will have nothing to do with it. She's said she's not saying it is true and she's not saying it isn't, she's just staying away from the whole issue. We avoid the whole subject if we can. We always have. And don't any of you bring it up either. But, listen, a few nights ago Sina told me something else about the night garden that Old Tom's aunt Bertha had once told them—a story Old Tom didn't want me to hear.

"'More than likely it's an old wives' tale,' Old Tom had said to Sina, 'and no point scaring the child by repeating it.'

"'But, Franny,' Sina said to me, 'I must tell you because Bertha saw a ghost, too. And she thought she knew whose it was.'"

Then I related to them what Sina had said to me.

"When Bertha was dying she finally told Old Tom and me about the ghost. It began with Maria May, who lived with her parents on East Sooke Farm. You can find her gravestone in the Sooke Cemetery, with the dates 1798–1822. She was known as a local beauty, but her marriage prospects weren't good. Her family hadn't much money, scratching a living on the farm. Then she fell in love with Captain Hawkins, a merchant seaman who came from a long aristocratic line in England. His first wife had died in childbirth and he would not marry again until the woman in question proved that she could carry a child to term and birth it successfully. So Maria May allowed herself to get pregnant out of wedlock. Before she could have the baby, the captain's father died and Captain Hawkins inherited the estate and returned to England to claim it, leaving a letter for Maria May saying that someday he would return for her. Maria May told her parents what had happened and begged her father to let her use her wish in the night garden to join Captain Hawkins and be happy. But her father forbade her any wish at all. He felt anyone who had gotten into the condition she had, hadn't the sense to make a decent wish. He told her to bide her time and he would think of a useful wish for her. Her happiness must be in his keeping from then on. Then, because her father had no doubt that Captain Hawkins would never return, he used his wish to wish him dead. When word came to them of Captain Hawkins's death, Maria May tried to use her wish to reverse her father's. She wrote to Captain Hawkins after that, hoping her wish had worked and he would reply, but instead she received a letter from relatives saying he was dead. When she told her mother about her letter and her last hope, her mother explained that no wish can be used to undo another's wish. It was the terrible finality of the night garden. The next morning Maria May's body was found washed up at the bottom of the cliff at Beechey Head.

"Her father said she had clearly gone mad and refused to acknowledge that he had taken all hope from her when he had taken control of her happiness. He said from then on he had no daughter and wiped her name from the family Bible and refused to have her buried on the farm as her mother wished. Her mother, full of remorse for not helping her daughter when she could have, had a stone erected in the Sooke Cemetery, but the coffin she buried beneath it was empty. Instead, she gave her husband a sleeping draught and secretly, with the help of the dairy maid, buried Maria May in the night garden, where she could gaze at her grave from her bedroom window on all the many nights thereafter when she couldn't sleep.

"But when this alone proved to be no solace, Maria May's mother took to sitting in the night garden night after night. Everyone, she thought, everyone is entitled to their own wish. No one is entitled to the control of another's happiness.

"The farmhands got used to seeing the lone figure out on the bench, staring into the evening, and then one morning they found her still there when the sun came up. She had used her wish to be with Maria May.

"'I'm telling you this, Franny,' Sina said to me, 'because I don't want to leave things unsaid like I did with the Space Institute man. When you told me you saw a ghost, I pretended not to believe you because I didn't want to. But that was cowardly. If Bertha saw a ghost, perhaps you did, too.'"

I was thinking I saw a ghost whether Bertha did or not but this was no time to be petty.

"'But was it Maria May's or her mother's?' I asked Sina.

"'Well, they say ghosts are the dead who cannot rest easy, so I think the mother's, myself. She, like I, regretted not speaking. Of course, it was only a UFO for me, nothing of great matter. Still, these things undone live on to be picked up by others.'

"'In the ether,' I said.

"'Just so. Like it or not we all drink from the same pond. Franny, I'm not saying any of this has even a crumb of truth. I am just laying it out there. The possibilities.'

"'There's the gravestone.'

"'Just so.'

"'And, of course . . .' I said.

"'The ghost,' said Sina."

Winifred was practically fainting from the effect of this story; she had collapsed half on and off my bed as if her legs could not support her. I thought at first it was the idea of ghosts that upset her, but then she whispered, "People will live in unhappiness for the love of others, won't they? People will do all manner of things for the love of others. Imprudent things! People will go to their *deaths* for the love of others."

Wilfred just pushed his glasses up his nose, unmoved, and said, "What about the hermit, then?"

"Well, when he got here, the night garden had been so neglected it was a mess of weeds, and little pine cones had blown in and it was in danger of being ruined by a crop of small ponderosa pines that were pushing their way up. Old Tom keeps the secret of the night garden, but when he invited the hermit to weed it, he had to explain the dangers to him."

"So did the hermit ever wish?" asked Winifred. "Even accidentally?"

"I don't know," I said.

"You'd better stay out of that garden," said Winifred, turning on Zebediah again.

"All right," said Zebediah. "But I'm going to go in and wish before we have to leave here. I can think of all kinds of things to wish for."

"What would *you* wish for, Wilfred?" I asked with sudden curiosity. Wilfred was a hard nut to crack personality-wise.

"A horse. No, a motorcycle," said Wilfred.

"I'd wish for a dozen, no, three hundred and sixty-five dresses, one for each day of the year," said Winifred, talking over Wilfred.

"You have nowhere to keep them," said Wilfred practically.

"Dresses, that's a stupid wish," said Zebediah. "You'd soon outgrow them."

"You wish for what you want, I'll wish for what I

want," said Winifred primly. "Anyhow, it's only pretend. The whole thing sounds cockeyed to me. I don't believe it for one instant. Still, if Old Tom says we can't wish, then we can't. It's his property and his garden and his rules, and don't you forget it, Zebediah."

"Oh, rules," scoffed Zebediah.

Then we heard the back door bang closed, and the Maddens scurried upstairs to bed before Old Tom could come upstairs and catch them in the hallway and maybe start yelling again, although I assured them that, tonight notwithstanding, he really hardly ever did.

I went back up to the cupola because once again I was wide awake. Although my mermaid story had been going great guns a while before, now it was as dead as a doornail. As I sat chewing on my pen, I saw a white blur drift through the Japanese garden. This blur was different in mass and shape from the one I'd seen in the dining room. Of course, I thought. Maria May haunts the *gardens*; Maria May's mother haunts the *house*. I was so overwhelmed with all that was happening that this seemed to make a kind of sense. I waved vaguely to her and went back to work, this time trying to write about ghosts, but that didn't go well either. Finally I just went to bed.

The next morning at breakfast, which Old Tom made because Gladys was taking her usual union-mandated Sunday off, there was a polite pall. I hadn't known such a thing existed until then. It was different from the pregnant pause even though both consisted of silence. Experiencing for the first time these pauses and palls was a definite side benefit of having different people in the house. In this pall you could clearly detect that Old Tom was going to pretend nothing had happened. Sina had managed to sleep through the whole debacle, and we children were not going to apprise her. Everyone was a bit more subdued, but by the time evening came and we'd had another wonderful roast chicken dinner with no burnt bits, we were all in a better mood and had a rousing hour around the piano. Gladys joined in without once bebopping, which seemed as miraculous as anything that had happened so far.

✦

Monday, Old Tom and Wilfred went out to weed the kitchen garden, Winifred and I went out to do the eggs,

Zebediah disappeared into the woods, and Sina came into the chicken coop and said, "Girls, I'm going to Brookman's, so could you load the truck for me?"

"Again?" I all but shouted.

"Yes," said Sina, looking shifty. "I, um, have another letter from Zebediah to mail."

Winifred and I looked at each other and rolled our eyes, but really I didn't see that there was anything we could do about this.

✦ ✦ ✦

The rest of the week continued the same: Zebediah disappeared, and Old Tom and Wilfred worked all day together. When I passed them, I heard:

"Beans."

"Trim ties."

"Carrot tops up."

"Bury tomato plants."

"Aphid control."

"Heliotrope?"

"Yep."

"Peas?"

"Too soon."

Then they began grunting. They seemed to have evolved a Morse code all their own consisting entirely of grunts, and whenever Old Tom passed Wilfred he gave him a little pat on the shoulder. I was happy for Old Tom if, as ever, a little jealous of Wilfred. After all, if Old Tom had needed help that badly all these years, he might have asked me. I felt guilty I hadn't intuited his need for help. Not that I wanted to spend my days sweating in the gardens—I knew what hard work it was—but still. One likes to be asked.

Gladys continued to make terrible food.

Winifred, Sina, and I hung out mornings at Brookman's.

Zebediah received a letter on Wednesday and Sina mailed his response on Thursday. Zebediah had told Sina we wanted to steal his mail. She was appalled, I'm sure, but all she said to me was, "Really, Franny, I wouldn't have thought it of you." She said nothing to Winifred, not wishing to be rude.

"Don't worry," growled Winifred to me later. "I'll find the letters."

But she looked and looked and couldn't find them, so Zebediah must have found a better hiding place.

✦ ✦ ✦

On Saturday, Sina announced we were once again going to Brookman's.

It was a quiet morning at the store; no one was there except for us, Mrs. Hornby, and Miss Macy. Mrs. Brookman was in the back doing inventory. As I watched, Sina, who had the radio turned up loud, started muttering to herself. I realized she was repeating bits and pieces of the things the radio announcer was saying. She was becoming more and more agitated. Miss Macy and Mrs. Hornby were sipping their coffees and listening as Sina, who seemed to have forgotten we were there, said, "Well, if there's something in that for me, I just don't get it. I just don't get it at all."

"Sina!" I said as light finally dawned. "You think the UFOs are trying to contact you via the radio. Just like Gladys said they would! You think they're speaking in code. You're trying to decipher it!"

And suddenly, instead of looking all haunted and upset, Sina stood up straight and dignified and said, "Nonsense."

"You are, too," I said. "That's why we've been coming so often."

"Well, I just don't *get* it." Sina broke down and wailed. "I'm not receiving any messages at all! Or if they are sending them to me, I am too stupid to understand. Why did they stop their spaceship outside my window? Why me? What are they trying to convey to me?"

"What spaceship?" asked Mrs. Hornby, and suddenly we remembered she and Miss Macy were standing right there, drinking coffee and listening in.

Mrs. Hornby was your typical tea-and-crumpet Englishwoman, the type who moves to Victoria from Britain and never gets rid of her tea cozies or her clipped accent. There are dozens of them. You're always tripping over them downtown so that if you didn't know, you would think this was some kind of colonial outpost instead of the Canadian provincial capital that it is. But Mrs. Hornby was better than most. She was kindly at least. She had the square body, square jaw, short hair, and sensible clothes of women of her ilk and looked as if there would be no nonsense about her. She's the person you'd go to if you needed a sudden tourniquet or the proper rules for a croquet match. She could, you felt, dispatch advice and medical help with a cool head in an emergency situation. She was not the type to whom you'd relate adventures with Martians. I could see all this running through Sina's head as she cocked it and looked into Mrs. Hornby's kindly inquisitive eyes. But then Sina surprised me. She seemed to visibly pull herself together and screw her courage to the sticking point, something she hadn't managed to do for the Space Institute man, so maybe she'd learned something that day. And almost defiantly she told the story of her spaceship.

I must admit, I was not so morally bold myself, and kind of hid behind Sina, peeking out now and then, unwilling to watch Mrs. Hornby's face assume a look of disgust as she cottoned on to the fact that Sina, formerly thought of as an upstanding member of the community, was revealed to be not merely wanting like Miss Macy but quite, quite mad. However, I was much mistaken, for instead of the look of disgust, Mrs. Hornby's eyes took on a troubled glazed expression as if she were puzzling something out and putting two and two together.

"I've never told another soul this," she said quietly. Then she put a hand confidingly on Sina's forearm, which startled us, it was so uncharacteristic; if there's one thing you can say for the Brits it's that they usually know how to keep their boundaries. "But something similar happened to me. About ten years ago. I was driving my granddaughter home from Brownies. And we were going down Lombard Road—you know that long avenue with all the poplars?"

We all nodded a bit frantically. We didn't want to break the spell.

"When suddenly the road ahead was flooded with light, and looking up I saw hovering not twenty feet over the road a giant spacecraft. It was perfectly circular, and covered in lights."

"Blue?" asked Sina sharply.

"I don't remember if they were blue. May have been. I just remember all the lights. And it simply hovered there. It was saucer-shaped, just like in the movies. That's when I knew I could never tell anyone. I couldn't believe it myself. What would my family in England say if they knew? Elspeth Hornby was seeing flying saucers. I pulled the car over. I was terrified, but, well, I don't know what else I was, enthralled, I guess, enchanted. Nothing like this had ever happened to me before. The world was suddenly as it was when I was a child and believed in fairies in the dell and such. What could it be doing here? In British Columbia? I said nothing about it to my granddaughter, who was in the backseat and didn't seem to notice. I said, 'Grandma just needs to get out and check the tires.' I didn't want to alarm her. And who knew if the aliens or whatever was in there were friendly. I got out and just stared up at it. I didn't know what else to do. And then it sped away in the blink of an eye. I've never seen anything move so fast in my life."

"Yes!" said Sina. *"Yes!"*

"Did you call the Canadian Space Institute?" I asked.

"No. As I said, I've never told anyone. And no one else has ever mentioned seeing such a thing to me. I've carried it in here." She pointed to her head, then her heart, then her head again. There seemed to be some confusion with Mrs. Hornby about where she was carrying it. "All these years."

Well, we stood there the way people do when gathered after a disaster, as if not knowing quite what to say about it, but being united by it all the same.

Then Miss Macy spoke. "I was a Brownie leader, you know. *Am* a Brownie leader."

We looked at her but said nothing. It was just like Miss Macy to start spouting non sequiturs at such a moment.

"I need to take the girls hiking and camping." Miss Macy went on as if we hadn't just heard the most extraordinary story. "Would you mind it if I took them on your property, Sina? It's so big, you see, and there must be so many promising places. And we could go for little practice hikes before camping to make sure the wee things are up to it. As you know, I walk there often myself, but I want to see how far my little troop can go."

"Uh, all right," said Sina and then jerked her shoulders straight as she came out of the spell.

"Yes, I must be off," said Mrs. Hornby and picked up her mail and trotted out, leaving us with dozens of unanswered and probably unthought-of questions.

But we hadn't time for them because Miss Macy went on, "You see, I'd really like to take them out soonish. The weather's so fine and they're out of school but will be back in school during the summer when we'd usually go. Would that be okay? Could I just come over now and then with a trial tyke when I get a second and do a little preliminary scouting?"

Two things occurred to me here. First, what did Miss Macy mean by "when I get a second"? As far as I knew, all she ever did was hang out at Brookman's and go for endless walks on our property. Did she mean take a break from her coffee breaks? Take time out from her long walks for a long walk? Second, it was amazing that anyone would entrust their daughter to her, especially to go on potentially dangerous hikes or overnight camping trips. But then again, I knew from bitter experience that no one ever wanted to be a Brownie leader. Our school had tried to get a Brownie troop going when I was seven, and no one, but no one, would come forward. Of course there was a war on. Women were having to take men's jobs as the men were shipped off to fight, so there were few left to tend the home fires let alone lead Brownies. And when they did get home from some job or other they had taken over for a man and had made dinner, helped with homework, done the laundry etc., the last thing they wanted to do was head out to the school gym to lead a bunch of seven-year-old girls in campfire songs and lecture them on the virtue of cookie sales. But apparently now they had Miss Macy. Maybe they were so grateful that if they lost a Brownie or two in the process they figured what the heck.

"Yes, that would be fine. I'll let Old Tom know," said Sina in a distracted tone, and then she got our mail. There was a letter to Zebediah there and when Sina put the mail down on the truck floor by my feet, my hand slid toward it but her hand automatically shot out and moved the mail to her side of the truck without her even losing her distracted expression. Sina's reflexes were stellar.

We drove silently down the road toward home, Sina's head obviously buzzing with yet another UFO sighting and the credence it lent to her experience and Gladys's prediction. Suddenly she did a U-turn right there on Sooke Road, which was not the safest thing, the road being full of blind curves and logging trucks usually. We survived it, however, even as the truck skidded about and Winifred and I hung on to each other for dear life. As the milk can beneath us, hardly big enough for the two of us, rolled and pitched, I said, "Where, may I ask, are we going?"

"To Victoria," Sina said in clipped, determined tones.

"Why?" I asked.

"To buy a radio," she said.

"What about the radio waves?" I sputtered through little yips of terror as the tires spun on gravel when Sina whipped around the curves.

"To heck with them," she said, gripping the wheel more tightly and stepping harder on the gas.

Once we got to Victoria we went immediately to Eaton's, where she asked for the radio department and we were directed upstairs. There a salesman pounced on us.

"Madam, can I help you?" he asked, swishing over in his shiny blue suit and patent leather shoes.

"That remains to be seen," said Sina. "I want a radio. A battery-powered radio."

"Of course," said the salesman.

"There's no of course about it," said Sina. "I've never wanted one before, and I doubt I shall ever again, but that is what I want at present."

"What were you looking for in a radio, madam, if I may be so bold?" asked the salesman. I guess he was used to dealing with all types, because Sina's whole demeanor implied a radio emergency of the most dire sort.

"Well, uh, something not too large," said Sina.

"Naturally," said the salesman.

"And, uh, something colorful would be nice."

"We have a stunning pink battery-powered model," said the salesman. "Bakelite."

"And, uh, something that picks up radio waves from far away."

"They all pick up radio waves from far away," chuckled the salesman. "If I may say so, that is the particular virtue of the radio. And, of course, all *our* radios are so blessed. Or perhaps 'talented' is a better word."

Sina ignored what would usually have been for us a heyday of ridiculous language to correct and the joys of edifying another clueless person about his native tongue. She had bigger fish to fry.

"No, I mean way far away," said Sina. "*Really* far away."

"I assure you, madam, our radios are equipped to be top of the line, best of the bunch, updated to the nth degree. You'll find no flaw with them. They pick up waves from so far, you'd be amazed."

"How amazed?" asked Sina flatly.

"What?" asked the salesman, beginning finally to falter.

"How far? Tell me how far and I'll tell you how amazed," said Sina.

"Did you want a precise distance? We can't give a precise distance, I am desolated to say." The salesman looked very, very sad. He had a long mustache. Somehow he made it droop.

"Yes, but approximately?"

"How far away did you have in mind?" countered the salesman, rallying.

"Outer space," said Sina. In for a crazy penny, in for a crazy pound.

"Ah, hahaha, I can see you're a trickster, that you are," said the salesman, laughing with his mouth but showing concern with the rest of his face.

"Yes, right, what about it, then? Can your radios get

waves from outer space?" asked Sina, looking down at him over her glasses.

Sina was so tall that when she did this, it occurred to you that from that height she could step on you if she chose. Or even eat you, if such an ogre-like urge should come upon her. It usually brought people around.

"Well, of course," said the salesman. "I'm certain it can, this lovely pink model, although, naturally, there is no way of testing this, as radio waves aren't sent from outer space, are they? Hahaha. But if they were sent from, uh, outer space, I'm sure this pink Bakelite model would do the job."

"Sina," I whispered, having spent this time studying all the price tags, "it's the most expensive one."

But the salesman must have heard me because he said, "That's because it's our *space* model." And he did a little flourish with his hand that was meant to convey the luxury nature of this radio. Or perhaps a flying saucer. It was difficult to tell.

"We'll take it," said Sina.

We drove home silently.

Sina carried the radio on her lap as if it were a baby.

And she must have been having second thoughts as she hauled it to her studio because when Old Tom came toward us to find out what had taken us so long and spied the radio, Sina said, "I don't want to talk about it."

Old Tom, who knew that tone, turned on his heel and went back to plant the cabbages, but Gladys, emerging from the house and also spying the radio, beamed from ear to ear.

"Finally!" she said.

The Letters

At lunch Sina gave Zebediah his letter and off he trotted upstairs, presumably to read it. Winifred and I were in near despair. If we followed him to steal it, he would only tell Sina again. We had come up with no other way to find out what was going on. Old Tom had told me once that even little children in France were doing dangerous jobs helping the French resistance. I couldn't help but feel that the Vichy regime would be doing happy slap-dancing if Winifred and I joined the French resistance.

After lunch, Gladys suggested that she and Sina listen to the radio together.

"I've been listening to it all week at Brookman's and ever since I got this one home," said Sina despondently. "I am ready to give it a break."

"What have you been listening to?" asked Gladys patiently.

"Oh, all kinds of things. Mostly the CBC," said Sina.

"That's your trouble right there," said Gladys. "You want to be listening to bebop."

"I do not," said Sina.

"You do. If you want to hear aliens, you need more music, less talk. Think about it. Why would a bunch of aliens connect with some channel that goes *blah blah blah blah blah blah blah blah*? They wouldn't. I wouldn't. We all have more sense. Bebop! That's the ticket. Something they can, you know, dance to in those flying machines of theirs."

"Are you suggesting," said Sina dangerously, "that Martians are hurling around through space snapping their fingers in time to the music?"

"If they've got fingers, they're snapping them," said Gladys, and stared down Sina defiantly.

Sina eyed her narrowly. "I am not convinced that the aliens will be speaking to me at all," she said. "But I am even more positive that if they do, it won't be musically. And if it were musically, it would not be bebop."

"I didn't say they'd be *singing* to you," said Gladys,

rolling her eyes. "The messages will be embedded in the music."

"And how do they expect me to de-embed them?" asked Sina.

"Ah well, that would be up to you, wouldn't it?" said Gladys challengingly.

"Yes, it would. I'm going to go listen to the CBC now. Alone. And you're going to get the baking done. See if you can't find something new to burn. Cornbread, perhaps."

"I'm sure I wouldn't burn things if I had some bebop in the kitchen," said Gladys.

"I'm sure you would," said Sina coldheartedly.

But this interesting debate was interrupted by a sudden knock on the door and the appearance of Miss Macy, who had come over to scout for good Brownie hikes and camping sites.

"Hello, this is little Ermintrude. She's my trial tyke. I'm taking her with me to see just how much her little legs can stand," said Miss Macy, pointing to an extremely nervous-looking six-year-old in full Brownie regalia.

"How do you do, Ermintrude," said Sina. "Well, have a nice hike." She waved them off airily. She had Martians to decode.

"I just thought I'd let you know I was going into the woods," Miss Macy went on. "That's good Girl Guide policy. Never go alone into the woods without telling someone."

"But you go off alone all the time without telling us. We see you," I said. But, of course, nobody paid any attention to me. Not when there were three, well, two adults and one half adult or whatever it was that Gladys qualified for, in the room.

"When might you return?" asked Sina, although she looked as if she didn't much care.

"I've no idea," said Miss Macy in surprise. "We're going to Beckman Cove to test the water temperature. If the water has gotten warm enough there, the girls may enjoy a paddle."

Beckman Cove was a small cove down our coast. Most of the waters in this part are so cold that swimming or even wading is out of the question, but there are a few coves where the ocean shelf is such that it is shallow a long way out and the water gets warmed there enough for swimming and wading. Beckman was one.

"How do you know about Beckman Cove?" I asked. "I know you walk here, but I didn't know you swam."

"One of the soldiers showed me," said Miss Macy. "They discovered it for swimming."

"Gosh darn it," said Sina. "It's one thing to have visitors in to play poker, but I draw the line at them showing people around our property as if it were theirs. And nobody said they could go swimming."

"But Miss Macy already has permission to walk everywhere," I said. "And it doesn't really disturb us if they swim, Beckman Cove is so far from the farm."

"That's not the point," said Sina stubbornly. "I'm happy to do my part for the war effort, but they're not to get cheeky and overstep their bounds."

"Yeah," said Gladys. "And where are all these soldiers? Soldiers everywhere, I was promised."

"Their barracks are right down the military road a piece," said Miss Macy.

"I didn't know you visited so often," said Sina.

"Oh, I don't know if I'd say often . . . now and again," said Miss Macy, looking shifty-eyed. "I get lonely."

Sina actually blushed and I think she wished she hadn't asked.

"Can you show me where?" asked Gladys.

"Girls, girls," said Sina. "We mustn't disturb the soldiers. They're clearly all too easily distracted. They're doing work for the war effort. Any distraction could land us in the drink. In hot water. In the soup. We mustn't interrupt their work."

"Oh, that's okay," said Miss Macy. "They're always looking for fresh poker players. There's only two of them kept manning the guns on the points here, and the rest are just there to trade shifts with them. I can tell you they are happy for any diversion. They get sick of each other."

"Nonsense," said Sina. "And I'm sure they do all kinds of important things they're too modest to mention. We mustn't bother them. We must support the war effort."

"Well, that's what I plan to do," said Gladys. "Lend my support. Come on, Miss Macy, let's go bring the boys some Girl Guide cookies."

"I'm very sorry, Miss Brookman, but we have no Girl Guide cookies on us. They're only sold at a certain time of year. We don't carry them in our pockets. No, we've got scouting to do. We must see how long little Ermintrude can walk before her legs completely collapse under her," said Miss Macy.

Ermintrude began to quiver.

"Anyhow," said Miss Macy, not noticing this, "you don't need me, Miss Brookman. Just head on down the road. You'll see their barracks eventually. Now my trial tyke and I will sally forth."

Miss Macy took off with little Ermintrude. Gladys, who was supposed to be baking, took off down the military road to visit the soldiers.

Sina clutched her head. It was clear that the population of the farm was increasing in dribs and drabs and was utterly out of control.

Meanwhile, Winifred and I could see Zebediah creeping down the stairs and sneaking out the back door.

Winifred jabbed me with a finger and whispered, "Come on. He's going to hide today's letter, I bet. Let's follow him."

So we sallied forth as well, staying at a distance and dodging behind buildings now and again until we reached the safe cover of the woods. From there it was easy. Zebediah would have made a rotten spy, because he didn't once cotton on to us. We stopped at one point when he got to the old petroglyphs. There are long, flat rocky ledges there where you can sun yourself and stare at the ancient rock pictures of seals. Zebediah sat down. Winifred and I squatted beneath a bush to watch as he took the letter out of his pocket, opened it, and read it before putting it back in his pocket and leaping up to carry on. He seemed to have a kind of spring in his step after that. Was it of suppressed excitement? Then he led us to the hermit's. The hermit was weeding his garden when Zebediah got there. We saw him show the hermit the letter, and the two of them disappeared into the hermit's cabin.

"He must be hiding the letters there," said Winifred.

"We need to find a way to lure the hermit out so we can search for them," I said. "But how?"

"I have it!" said Winifred so loudly I was afraid she had given us away. Then she motioned for us to head back to the house. We'd walked a bit when she said, "Don't you see? We don't have to lure him away at all. We'll go there tonight by cover of nightfall when the hermit comes to weed the night garden. Does he come every night?"

I thought about this. "Not every night, but he often comes whenever the moon is bright," I replied. "But even with a bright moon it will be pitch black on that trail through the forest and easy enough to fall over the cliffs."

"We'll carry flashlights," said Winifred.

"Which will attract the cougars that prowl at night."

"Well, no plan is perfect," said Winifred.

I looked at her to see if she was joking, but she turned

to me a face bereft of fun and games and said, "I'm terribly worried about Father, Franny. Terribly."

"So it's a plan," I said.

✦ ✦ ✦

That night the sky was so thickly covered in clouds that the moon wasn't visible and the hermit never came. So we waited patiently for Sunday night, hoping the skies would clear and doing our best to appear normal with such plans in the offing. We ate Gladys's terrible cooking. She had decided to try making the Sunday chicken. She claimed she had a better recipe than Old Tom's. We all begged Old Tom to overrule her and make the chicken himself, but he said we must give her a chance to shine, which was very like him. So we crossed our fingers and hoped she really did have a good recipe, but it turned out to be scorched chicken and dumplings.

"How in the world," said Sina, more in wonder than criticism, "do you manage to scorch dumplings? They're made in liquid."

"Not always," said Gladys, who invariably ate her own cooking with relish.

Gladys had spent the afternoon first visiting the soldiers with offerings of burnt cookies, which she claimed they liked just fine, then slumped against the outside of Sina's studio listening to the radio and periodically calling out, "Change the station," to which Sina would reply, "Go away," before Gladys finally did in order to make dinner.

After dinner we sang around the piano as the moon shone brilliantly through the window and Winifred and I nodded meaningly at each other.

We sang gospel hymns and the entire score of *Oklahoma!*, the big smash-hit Broadway musical. Gladys kept trying to insert bebops between the lines of "Many a New Day" and "I Cain't Say No." Sina looked vaguely perturbed by this rendition—"Many a New Day" lost some of its innocent charm, it was true, when it was sung by a slouched and finger-snapping Gladys inserting *bebop bebop* every other line—but everyone was feeling so fine and full of energy that no one was small-minded enough to carp about this. Because everyone was having a good time, it took forever until people were willing to drift off to bed. I finally got the ball rolling by yawning loudly and theatrically. I find this is contagious and will often get recalcitrant bedgoers in the mood. Indeed, soon people began to yawn with me and stretch and complain of their terrible fatigue and it was all I could do not to shout *Then go to bed!*

Eventually everyone did drift off to their own quarters. Winifred sneaked into my room, and together we waited fully dressed for everyone to fall asleep and the hermit to make his way into the night garden. We were sitting at the window in the dark staring at where the fields ended and the woods began, watching as Gladys, with a flashlight, headed down the military road, and looking for the hermit to arrive when Sina knocked at my door.

Winifred and I stared mutely horrified at each other.

Finally I croaked, "Yes?"

"It's Sina, dear, can I come in?" she said.

"No!" I said, without thinking. "That is, I'm almost asleep, Sina."

"No, you're not. I can tell from where your voice is. You aren't in bed—you're by the window, aren't you?"

"No, I'm just throwing my voice," I said. "It's a trick Winifred taught me."

"Why would she teach you to throw your voice?" asked Sina. "It seems a silly thing to do."

"She just did," I said, discovering that in a pinch I had

no talents as a liar. I am not one of those sorts who can make up long and elaborate stories at the drop of a hat. "People do do things just because, you know."

"Yes, true, very true," said Sina. "It's just that I've been missing you lately. Since the Onslaught." (Which was how Sina had been secretly referring to the arrival of all these people.) "We've stopped rocking on the landing and watching the sunsets together, you and I."

"I know. I miss it, too," I said, my heart suddenly bleeding for Sina. And although I'd been too busy, really, to miss it until now, as she mentioned it, I began to miss it, too. It was tempting to throw Winifred out and pull Sina in. All my life Sina and I had been in the habit of sharing our sunset hour. But no, Winifred was terribly worried about her father. Her need was real. I must not abandon her.

"So I thought I would come in and spend a little time. I don't want to go to the landing because lately my experience is that as soon as we alight somewhere we are suddenly crawling with people the way an open honey jar collects ants. But I thought I'd pay you a little visit in here, where no one would find us."

"That would be nice, Sina," I said while Winifred

pinched me and shook her head, "but I'm, as I said, almost asleep. Let's do it tomorrow."

But oh, I thought, these bonds of intimacy we have with our friends, based so often on loyalty and habit and the type of good talk I can always count on with Sina, can so easily be destroyed in a second by misunderstanding. It would level me if so it went for Sina and me.

"Well..." said Sina. "Just let me come in and say goodnight, then."

"The door is locked," I said. That much was true. Winifred had locked it. Thank goodness one of us had foresight. "And I'm too tired to open it."

"Oh," said Sina. I could hear her backing away. And again my heart broke for her. She really was, for such a towering person, very sensitive. "All right then. Well, good night."

"Good night, Sina," I said.

There was quiet and we could hear her walking away and saying to herself in low tones, "They outgrow you. Of course, they do."

I called through the door. "I'll never outgrow you, Sina." But she had already gone into her own room and I heard her door close and I don't think she heard me.

"Never mind," said Winifred, who, in her own way, was quite single-minded and heartless. "She'll get over it. Look, there's the hermit."

And sure enough he was making his way across the field, and then he opened the gate to the night garden.

"He doesn't climb over the fence, he uses a *key*!" I said, outraged. "How did he get a key? Old Tom said that lock has been rusted shut for years."

"Old Tom lied," said Winifred, again with the heartless devotion to her purpose. I was beginning to regret my choice of compeers for the night assault on the hermit's cabin. But it was too late now. We slipped soundlessly out of the house. The hermit was busy in the garden, so we crept across the fields by moonlight and didn't turn on our flashlights until we got to the woods.

The woods at night are a different thing. Full of shadows and rocks and roots to trip you up. It took twice as long as usual to reach the hermit's and often one or the other of us wanted to turn back, but we persevered, driven by Winifred's terrible anxiety for her father. And when finally we got there we were glad we had come, for we went immediately into his cabin and the letters sat on a table, not even hidden. We read them in the order we found them:

1. NOW IS THE TIME.

"Oh," said Winifred, "Mother said that Daddy was going to do something stupid. She must have known it was the time for a stupid thing. I should never have doubted her. I'm an idiot."

"You are not an idiot, Winifred," I said staunchly. "You were merely a person with insufficient information. Now let's read the rest of the letters and figure out what is being communicated between Zebediah and your father that is such a big secret."

2. BE CAREFUL.
3. KEEP IT TO YOURSELF BUT FIND OUT MORE.
4. ASK HIM TO TELL YOU THE CODE.
5. MONDAY IS THE DAY. IF I DON'T SEE YOU AGAIN, TELL EVERYONE I LOVE THEM.

Winifred just stood holding the last as if turned to stone.

I was the one who spoke. "It's worse than we thought."

Radio Reports

We shot out of the cabin, clutching the letters and stumbling down the dark path. Luckily, the hermit was still working in the garden, so we didn't run into him.

"Why a code? What code?" I said over and over. "Ask who for the code?"

"How should I know?" said Winifred. "None of it makes sense. There's no point asking Zebediah again. If he read that last letter and it awoke no terror in his heart, then I think it's safe to say we will never find out anything from him. There is only one thing to do. Wilfred and I will have to call Mother. We can pass on what we know and alert her to the dangers ahead. And, most important, we can tell her that tomorrow is *the day,* whatever that means. Unless this is all just some kind of big joke or big make-believe game between Father and Zebediah."

"Yes, of course," I said. "Surely it is only that."

"You don't know Father," said Winifred worriedly. "But we can tell Mother and let her sort it out."

"Yes, we'll get Sina to take us all to Brookman's in the morning and you can call your mother," I said.

We hurried the rest of the way to the house. And having decided on a plan of action, we went to bed. I slept well thanks to the unusual evening exercise. I cannot speak for Winifred, whom I assume was prey to the tossing and turning experienced by those who are being anguished by their inconsiderate loved ones.

+ ✦ +

The next morning we came down to breakfast and, sure enough, Winifred's normally long and well-brushed hair was in rats and knots all over her head. When Gladys saw it, she startled visibly.

"Gee," she said, "maybe I *should* lend you one of my beauty magazines."

I refrained from saying that her beauty magazines

didn't seem to have done much for her. Gladys's hair was a museum of past meals.

Winifred and I were a bit late for breakfast, as we had risen later than normal. Sina had already breakfasted and was in her studio. Zebediah had made for the woods, and we assumed Old Tom and Wilfred were out working in one of the gardens. The plan was to alert Wilfred, explain things, and then beg Sina to take us to Brookman's to make the call. But when we got outside, Old Tom and Wilfred were nowhere to be found. We checked the cows, the pig sty, the barn, the gardens, the potato field, and the orchard and then tromped from one hayfield to the next. Nothing.

"This farm has too many fields," I grumbled as we traversed the length and breadth of it.

Finally we gave up and went to the studio. Gladys was slouched against the outside wall calling, "This is an alien speaking. Change the channel to bebop."

"Go away, Gladys," Sina called back.

"Where are Old Tom and Wilfred?" we asked, charging inside.

Sina was walking around and around a new version of her mermaid. This one had horns.

"I've never heard of a mermaid with horns," I said.

"I thought horns might help," said Sina. "But you're right. It's rubbish. It doesn't matter anyhow—horns or not, it's not *that* which I'm trying to capture. Why can't I capture *it*? Why?" And she knocked the whole thing to the ground and jumped on it.

"What are you trying to capture?" asked Winifred tremulously. It is unnerving to see a large woman jumping up and down on clay.

"Something. That which cannot be named," said Sina. "Or defined. Or *here*!" She turned up the volume on the radio. "It's Mozart's Divertimento in D Major. The Andante."

We all stood transfixed. The music had such aching longing. And it seemed to pull into music what one so often felt but couldn't name.

"It's no bebop!" called Gladys. "And what's with those CBC guys that they have to play this same piece constantly?"

"You be quiet," said Sina. Then she shook it off. "Old Tom took Wilfred fishing. He said they might not be back until tomorrow. If the water's not too choppy, he thought he might go up the coast and stay at Friday Harbor. He says Wilfred deserves a holiday and they're way ahead on the gardens now."

"Noooooo!" said Winifred.

Sina just looked at her inquiringly. All along she had been expecting some version of the Crying Alice influence to out.

"We need to tell Wilfred something," explained Winifred, beginning to breathe too rapidly.

"Well, you've no choice but to wait. We can't recall them from the ocean, you know. What are your plans for today? Have you gathered the eggs yet?"

"Not yet. We'll get back to you about our plans," I said, dragging Winifred outside to discuss the situation.

"We have to do something," she said, still breathing quickly and her eyes beginning to bulge.

"Well, fine," I said, grabbing her arm and giving her a little shake in hopes of getting her to collect herself. "We don't need Wilfred to call your mother. Let's go back in and tell Sina everything."

"No," said Winifred, taking her arm back.

"Winifred, you must settle on *some* course of action," I said.

"Oh dear, but it's all so difficult. I think we must tell Mother, and then again I think we mustn't sound an alarm until we are sure something is afoot. Zebediah and Father could be having some kind of game for all we know."

"We've been through all this. Your mother knows something is afoot or she wouldn't have gone up to Comox, yes? It won't be a shock for *her*," I said. "I say we call her and read her the letters."

"I don't know," said Winifred. "I wish Wilfred were here."

Really, I thought. I was suddenly glad I had no brother if one became so dependent upon his judgment.

"Perhaps we should ask the hermit what is up. Maybe Sina could ask him. He would have to tell *her*," said Winifred.

"He wouldn't," I argued. "And she would be hard-pressed to ask him. She believes everyone should mind their own business."

"But not in an emergency surely?" said Winifred.

"She'd say if it's an emergency we must call your mother."

"Oh, I don't know what to do. I don't know what to do," said Winifred.

I knew what I thought she should do, but the problem was I wasn't really privy to the ins and outs of her family. And she didn't know mine. And nobody really knew the hermit. It was a delicate dance of conflicting constellations of people, all with their different star formations, their patterns of light and dark and gravitational pulls.

"I'll tell you what, let's gather the eggs," I said. "I find that doing something manually often helps to unstick you mentally."

So we gathered the eggs and then Sina kept finding us small chores to do, which if I were a pettier person, I might think had something to do with me not letting her come in to say good night the night before. We'd just finished sweeping the porch when Miss Macy showed up with a new trial tyke.

"This is Cheryl," she said to us.

"Hello, Cheryl," said Sina. "Where is your previous trial tyke?"

"Bit of a washout, that one. Buckled after only six kilometers. Didn't even want to come on the campout after that. But I'm sure she'll be fine when they're done rehydrating her," said Miss Macy. "In the meantime, Cheryl here is made of stouter stuff, aren't you, Cheryl? No mere rappelling down cliffside and scrambling over bear dens will extinguish your Brownie bravado, will it?"

Cheryl began to shake. It was becoming the familiar Brownie tell.

"I thought not," said Miss Macy before Cheryl had a chance to answer. "We're off to build a fire ring on the site Ermintrude and I found Saturday. There's a lot to do to prepare for the campout! Onward. Onward we go with compass and bow!"

That is when I noticed they were both wearing bows across their backs.

"Aren't Brownies a little young for archery?" I asked, raising my eyebrows.

"You are never too young to defend yourself against a *wild beast*!" said Miss Macy.

"I hope you brought water this time," said Sina faintly.

Normally she would have said nothing. She wanted nothing to do with the hearty Girl Guide promulgation, but she didn't want a property full of small children blowing about like tumbleweeds either.

Winifred and I went back to pacing up and down the length and breadth of the farm, Winifred waffling between wanting to call her mother, wanting to choke the information out of Zebediah, wanting to threaten the hermit, and wanting to wait and hope for the best.

"If Zebediah has gone to see the hermit, he must know by now that we took the letters," I said.

"Or he suspects the hermit has done away with them. Zebediah is very suspicious. He has never been a trusting soul," said Winifred worriedly, and picked up the pace. It was an unusually hot day. I sweated, stumbling along behind her, hoping she would come to a conclusion before I looked like a trial tyke myself.

"All right, let's tell Mother," said Winifred finally when we'd completed our eighth lap of the fields.

"That would have been my choice," I said.

I wanted to add that if she'd chosen to do that back when I had, while still on lap number one, she would have saved us considerable wear and tear on our sneakers; but, of course, I did not say this, as Winifred had enough to contend with.

We were therefore startled when approaching Sina's studio to see her flying out of it, radio in hand, screeching, "Oh dear! Oh dear! Franny, darling, come quickly! Winifred, Zebediah!"

We ran to her and she said nothing more, but thrust the radio out in front of us while turning up the volume.

"And the *Argot*, the air force's long-distance reconnaissance plane, has been stolen from the air base in

Comox. The *Argot* is known to be coveted by other countries for its ability to fly for days without refueling. A maintenance man, Robert Madden, is missing as well. Whether he has been kidnapped or has himself something to do with the plane's disappearance is unknown at this point."

"*That's* what this has been about? He's *stolen a plane*? Mother must know. That's what she must have meant by saying he was going to do something stupid," Winifred wailed, and then she finally satisfied Sina's every secret prognostication by breaking into sobs every bit as hysterical and racking as Crying Alice's.

Sina and I could think of nothing to say to comfort her. And before we could, a car came barreling down the farm road, nearly running us over in its urgency. It came to a crunching crash right beside us, and out leapt Mrs. Brookman. "Oh good, dear," she said, running up to Winifred and clutching her by the shoulders. "Quickly. Your mother called the store and wants you children to call her back. Where are your brothers?"

Through her wails Winifred said, "Wilfred is fishing . . . *sob sob* . . . not back until we don't *know when* . . . *sob sob sob* . . . and Zebediah is somewhere in the woods . . . *sob sob sob cough sob cough* . . . with a *hermit*."

She said the last as if Zebediah had purposefully chosen the most ridiculous companion possible out of pure spite.

"Zebediah!" said Sina. "If he comes home for lunch while we're gone, he'll be worried. I'll leave him a sandwich and a note saying we're at Brookman's. There's no point telling him about his father until we learn more."

She dashed inside while Mrs. Brookman turned once more to Winifred. "I'm so sorry, my dear. I guess it's up to you alone to make the call . . ."

We waited impatiently until Sina came back outside. Then Mrs. Brookman said to Winifred, who looked stunned, "Come, there's no time to waste," and hustled us to her car.

"The phone call—was it about the *olenstay aneplay*?" Sina asked Mrs. Brookman.

"Well, what else could it be about? Oh, poor, poor Mother," sobbed Winifred, amazing us all with her easy acquisition of a foreign language, even if it was only pig latin.

"Now, now," said Mrs. Brookman. "We know nothing at this point. Your father's disappearance could be a coincidence."

"Ha. Fat chance," said Winifred, and then began sobbing again.

"Winifred, dear," said Sina. "Do you know something we don't?"

I pinched Winifred. I thought it best that if Winifred's father were truly in trouble, as it was now clear that he was, that we not get him further in trouble by divulging what we knew. Not to mention what kind of trouble we might be in for having had some advance inkling of it without doing anything about it.

We rode in silence except for Winifred's sniffles. Sina brought the radio with us and kept it tuned to the CBC waiting for the next news break. It was interesting riding in a car with the radio playing.

"Someday," I said as I began to find our silence awkward and just trying to make cheerful conversation, "they should put radios in cars."

"Hush, Franny, not now," said Sina.

"They do put radios in cars, dear," said Mrs. Brookman kindly. "But your farm truck is an old 1918 Buick, and this is a 1927 Nash touring car. They didn't put radios in cars until about a decade ago."

I was put out to think that once again somebody had beaten me to the punch of a groundbreaking invention. Oh well, I wasn't an inventor. I was a writer. That was difficult enough.

"Sssssh!" said Winifred fiercely as the news came on again. They were interviewing Crying Alice.

"How could he have?" came her voice over the radio. "He's not a real pilot. He's just read about it! He's been so strange and edgy of late, but I never expected *this*."

"Oh, Mother!" shouted Winifred in supreme irritation. "What a thing to say!"

We shushed her as Crying Alice continued to rant to the interviewer. "I came up to Comox because I thought he was going to do something stupid. I have a sixth sense about these things. And when I got here he said to me, 'I plan to do something spectacular, life-changing, life-threatening even, something bold and beautiful and I can't tell you what it is.'

"'You must tell me,' I begged him over and over, 'You must tell me if it's life-threatening. Could you die?'

"'I could,' he said.

"'Then tell me.'

"'No can do,' he said. 'You would only try to talk me out of it.'

"That man can be so maddening!"

"So, Mrs. Madden, do you think then that your husband was talking about stealing the *Argot*?"

There was a horrified pause in which it was evident

that Crying Alice had just realized what she had copped to. "No," she replied. But it was clear she was lying.

"Oh, Mother!" cried Winifred. "Why can't you *think* before you speak?"

"Your mother seemed quite upset on the phone," said Mrs. Brookman. "She was *crying*."

Sina and I glanced at each other but, of course, didn't comment on this.

Nobody said anything else, but Winifred drew herself up and got a steely look. If her mother wasn't going to stand by her father, Winifred was. When we got to Brookman's, Mrs. Brookman dialed the number she had been given and gave the phone receiver to Winifred.

"Mother," said Winifred tentatively.

"Waaaaaaaaah!" came the cry from from the other end.

"Now, Mother, pull yourself together. Father may be just fine. He may have, um, just gone for a walk. Or a drive. There's no *evidence*."

"Waaaaaah!"

"Whatever he did or did not do, I'm sure he did or did not do it for a good reason. We must stand by him, Mother, not go giving unhelpful interviews to radio people."

"Waaaaaah!"

"All right. Well, I'm glad we had this talk. We're all just fine here. Why don't you call again when you have news or when you're better equipped to keep up your end of the conversation."

"Waaarrrrr waarrrrrr waarrrrrr!"

Crying Alice's cries had taken on the unexpected addition of a burred *r*. She was a bit like an engine revving up. But what this presaged, we could not imagine.

"Good-bye, Mother," said Winifred hastily and hung up.

She frowned for a second, her forehead all furrowed. We frowned, too, in commiseration.

"Well," Winifred said finally, "she's going to be no help. That much, I'm afraid, is clear."

"What would you like to do, dear?" asked Sina.

"Go home," said Winifred. "That is, to your home. Go home and wait for Zebediah and Wilfred."

"Yes, of course," said Sina.

Mrs. Brookman drove us back, the radio on the whole time, but there was no further news. We thanked Mrs. Brookman when we reached home and got out. We were almost at the door when she called through her car window, "By the way, how is Gladys working out?"

"Wonderfully!" called Sina back. There was enough misery that day without creating more.

And miserable it was. We might just as well have stayed at Brookman's because three more times that day Crying Alice called Mrs. Brookman and Mrs. Brookman came to fetch Winifred. The first time was when the newscast said, "Planes have been dispatched to search for the *Argot*, but Lieutenant Colonel McGee, in charge of the operation, when asked if they expect to find the *Argot*, would say only, 'It's a big ocean out there.'" But when Winifred called her mother from Brookman's, all Crying Alice would do was sob into the phone.

The second time was when the newscast reported, "There is a suspicion now that the bomber has onboard a crew of Japanese spies. 'Those Japs are sneaky types,' said Lieutenant Colonel McGee. 'I wouldn't put much past them. And for all we know, Robert Madden is their inside man.'"

When Winifred phoned her mother she said levelly, "Mother, you must not believe everything you hear."

Crying Alice's helpful and elucidating response was, *"Waaaah!"*

The last time was after we heard that air force planes

were now being told that if they came upon the *Argot*, they were to shoot to kill.

Winifred turned chalky white at this and returned her mother's call. "Oh, Mother," she whispered into the phone.

Her mother's comforting response was, *"Sniffle, sniffle, sniffle, waaaah!"*

Because she had no family to support her, Winifred became coldly capable. After the third trip to Brookman's she said to me, "Come on," and pulled me outdoors. We had been sitting in the dining room with Sina, listening to the radio. None of us saying anything, taking turns pacing or looking out the window for the return of Wilfred or Zebediah.

"And we thought ghosts were frightening," I said bitterly as Winifred dragged me through a field. "Where are we going?"

But Winifred just led the way out to the woods and along the coastal path until we got to the petroglyphs. There Winifred pulled her father's letters out of her pocket as well as a book of matches.

"We must burn these," she said.

Good thinking, Winifred!

"It's lucky we didn't tell Mother about them. She would have broadcast it all over Canada. And when Zebediah returns we must impress upon him that he is to say *nothing* of his correspondence with Daddy. They are shooting to kill." She said the last without emotion, which is when I learned that sometimes when great emotion is at hand, little is expressed.

We burned the letters, and I must say it was a welcome reprieve from pacing around the dining room and waiting for more newscasts, but, of course, we went right back to it after that. There was no one in her family left to monitor the situation except Winifred and she was doing a darned fine job.

Afternoon drifted into evening. Gladys, who had been apprised of the situation, came in and out with tempting little charred treats, which I thought unusually sensitive of her, and she did not ask us to change the channel to bebop once.

At dinnertime none of us felt like eating, but at least we could count on the return of Zebediah, who had eaten his sandwich and left again while we were at Brookman's and so was still in the dark. Sina had one hard-and-fast rule: we might wander wherever we liked during the day, but mealtimes must be observed. It was a way, as much as anything, of checking in so that she knew we hadn't drowned ourselves or been eaten by bears. So we knew Zebediah would be in for dinner soon and sure enough, just as Gladys was about to put it on the table we saw him coming from the woods. Then, to our relief, from the other direction, we spied Old Tom and Wilfred bringing the boat in. We let Zebediah come in and wash up without telling him anything, waiting for Wilfred. When everyone was together and had sat down at the table we told all.

Wilfred turned white and said nothing.

Zebediah, however, convulsed those of us who had been white-knuckling it through the day by standing on his chair, punching a fist to the heavens, and calling out gleefully, *"He did it!"*

Into the Night

Zebediah, sit down," said Sina with great restraint, I thought. She looked at Winifred and Wilfred's drawn faces and continued, "Now, I know this looks bad . . ." And then could clearly think of no good way to end her sentence, so she said, "Would anyone like a little charred soup?"

Gladys had brought in the soup tureen, from which came the distinct smell of burnt tomatoes.

"What are we going to do?" asked Wilfred calmly but looking owl-like and mildly panicked behind his glasses.

"We are going to eat soup," said Sina. "It will do no good to starve to death. Now, I think it best that, should anyone decide to ask us, that we know nothing about the missing plane. Not that we do."

"Zebediah, you are to keep your lips zipped," said Winifred. "They are talking about shooting to kill."

"What are we going to do?" asked Wilfred again.

"You're going to eat dinner and go to bed," said Old Tom. "There is nothing more you can do."

"Yes," said Sina, getting all falsely cheerful. "That's much the best thing. We are assuming that Zebediah actually knows something—"

"I do," interrupted Zebediah.

"You shut up," said Winifred rudely.

"I will not," said Zebediah.

"You both shut up," said Wilfred with unusual heat. "And let Sina speak."

"Thank you, Wilfred," said Sina. "What I was going to say was that, after all, we don't know that your father *has* done anything, what Zebediah thinks he knows aside. It could still all be talk. I always find the best way to deal with anything is with a clear head, and you won't have a clear head worrying all night. Try to have cheerful thoughts and get some rest."

"I want to hear the radio reports," said Wilfred. "Notwithstanding."

"Oh, now, dear, that may not be the best," said Sina. "Radio men and news people always try to create a stir. They want to keep you listening because that's how they get sponsors, and getting sponsors is how they make money. So you cannot rely on anything they say whatsoever. Why don't you let Tom and me listen and we'll come and get you if there's any real news."

"No, thank you," said Wilfred. "That's very kind, but I won't sleep anyway. I want to hear the reports myself."

Sina wrung her hands, but she turned on the radio, saying, "Anyone for dessert?"

There were no takers, but Gladys brought in the burnt cherry cobbler anyway and placed it in the middle of the table like some kind of sacrificial lamb. She stared sadly at it, trying to appear as aggrieved as the rest of us, although it was clear that some part of her found the state of affairs very exciting.

"I've never lived in a house with relatives of someone most likely about to be hanged for treason," she said, and ate three portions of the cobbler with gusto while Sina glared at her.

We sat for an hour and the news came in bits and pieces. At first it seemed it was much the same. Then the commentator said, "We have been told that the *Argot* can only be started by a handful of people in Canada who know the security access code. This code must be punched into a keyboard on the panel of the plane. If Robert Madden did start the plane or is working with enemy Japanese agents, they must have somehow managed to break the code. Alternatively, whoever stole the plane had help from someone with access to this information. And as there are only a very few people with this information, they are being interviewed, but none of them are as yet a suspect. Although Robert Madden is suspected of being part of the mysterious disappearance of the *Argot*, he was only maintenance and would not have been privy to the top-secret *Argot* access code. And we do not know where he is, so the military says that while his disappearance is suspicious, nothing can be confirmed at this time."

"There, you see," said Sina. " 'Nothing can be confirmed.' "

"Father couldn't have known the access code," said Wilfred. "So the question is, where is he?"

"Yes, he could have known the access code," said Zebediah excitedly.

"The letters!" said Winifred. "Father said to you in one letter, ask *him* for the code. Who? Ask who?"

"The hermit," said Zebediah importantly. "Father always wanted to fly the *Argot*. I was telling the hermit about it, and he said he knew how. And he told me there was a code to start the plane. He told me what it was and helped me print it correctly, and I sent it to Father."

"And I thought the hermit wouldn't bother with a twitchy little boy," I said, and then realized this was rude even under the circumstances. "Sorry, Zebediah."

"I told you he thinks I'm special," said Zebediah.

"You are not! I never heard of such a thing!" said Winifred.

"Father always wanted to fly the *Argot*?" said Wilfred.

"Yes. He told me when we lived in Comox. He said day after day after day he goes in and takes care of the plane. But he doesn't want to take care of planes; he wants to fly them. They won't let him be a pilot because he never got his high school diploma. Which is very unfair. He *knows* how to fly a plane. He said he knows the *Argot*. He *loves* the *Argot*. He said he just wanted to take it up *once*. To see what it was like. He said he planned to do it and bring it right back. He decided now was the time, that he was going to try to break the code. He had a plan to push a different series of numbers until he hit upon the right sequence. But then the hermit gave me the code and I gave it to Father. So now he gets his chance to fly it. You don't have to worry. He was never planning on stealing it. They got that part all wrong. He just wants to play with it."

"Well, if he just wanted to play with it," said Winifred, "why hasn't he returned it yet?"

"Maybe he's having fun!" said Zebediah. "I want to go up, too!"

"No you don't!" snapped Wilfred.

"Me too!" said Gladys. But we ignored her. She had absentmindedly polished off the rest of the cobbler while hanging on every thrilling word.

"Yes I do. I want to play with the *Argot* with Daddy," said Zebediah stubbornly. He stood up on his chair, held his arms out, and began to make his airplane buzzing noises.

"Sit down!" ordered Winifred. "Don't you get it, Zebediah? The air force doesn't let people *play* with their planes."

"And the hermit?" said Wilfred. "Did you hear the man on the radio say that only a handful of people in Canada know the access code? The hermit couldn't possibly know it."

"Well, I guess he does," said Zebediah smugly. "Because Father is gone and so is the plane."

At this, I think it is safe to say everyone's blood froze. Because, of course, Zebediah was right. We could no longer believe it was a coincidence that Fixing Bob and the plane were both gone. Our last hope had been that Fixing Bob had no way to get the plane going without the access code. But if the hermit had really given it to him, then Fixing Bob was in it up to his eyebrows. And, who knows, perhaps all the Maddens would be arrested as spies. And who was the hermit or who had he been to have access to the security code of Canada's most top-secret surveillance plane?

"I'm going to go talk to the hermit," said Old Tom, standing up. "Turn the radio off, Sina. Leave the dishes for morning, Gladys, and go to your cabin. Children, go to bed."

Old Tom seldom gave orders, and it startled us. Sina turned the radio off with a smart snap of the dial and then said, "Yes, off you go, children. There's no more to be done here tonight."

"But we'll never sleep," said Winifred.

"I'll bring you some hot milk with chamomile," said Sina.

She and Old Tom suddenly seemed very grown-up in a way they weren't usually. And very efficient and decided, not their old dozy selves at all. "Come on, now, off you go to think cheerful thoughts," said Sina. "If there's any news at all, I will wake you, but there's no point staying up for no news."

Old Tom had already put on his heavy wool shirt and taken his flashlight. We could see its progression across the fields. We went to our rooms. I was going to offer to let Winifred stay with me that night, but I could tell that the Maddens were stunned and not in the mood for chitchat of even the most sympathetic sort.

I was lying in bed listening to the sounds of Sina stoking the stove, rattling pans, heating up milk, and getting out cups when suddenly I heard something else. Feet padding across the floor and down the stairs.

What in the world? I said to myself, and when the back door banged, I went to the window and saw Zebediah running barefoot toward the night garden. Before I had time to do anything, he had climbed like a monkey up the fence and hoisted himself over to the other side. Once in the garden, which was glowing in the moonlight, he stood for just one second before disappearing. He was simply gone completely. Vanished into thin air.

I ran upstairs to Winifred's room. She was in bed, staring at the ceiling and clearly not thinking the cheerful thoughts she had been ordered to think.

"What?" asked Winifred.

"Zebediah . . ." I began.

"Yes, I know," said Winifred. "He told us he was going to the outhouse."

"Well, he didn't," I said. "He went to the night garden. I mean, actually *into* the night garden, and then he disappeared."

Winifred and I raced into Wilfred's room, where I repeated all this to him.

"What do you mean?" asked Wilfred. "Do you mean he then took off for the woods?"

"No, he never *left* the night garden. I mean, one second he was there and the next he was gone. I saw it all out my bedroom window."

"Nonsense," said Wilfred. "He must have ducked behind a statue or something."

"No," I said. "I'm telling you. I saw it. He vanished into thin air."

"That's impossible," said Wilfred.

He was irritated and I knew how he felt. Magic is all right when you're bored and want to pretend something more interesting. But when you're in crisis and your resources are stretched to the breaking point, you really don't want to be bothered with such nonsense. You want the security of a solid, familiar reality and the grounded earthbound things you know. But facts are facts. And sometimes you have to deal with what is in front of you whether you want to or not.

"I think he wished," I said. "I think he wished and his wish took him somewhere."

"Ridiculous," said Wilfred.

But Winifred looked stunned and terrified as the realization hit her.

"If he wished," she whispered to herself, "what would he wish for?"

Then, before we could stop her, she screamed, "Zebediah!" and went tearing out of the room and down the stairs.

"What bunk," said Wilfred, but still chased after her while I raced after Wilfred.

"Winifred!" cried Wilfred.

By the time Wilfred and I got outside, Winifred was already over the fence and then, to our horror, she disappeared, too. Wilfred had to believe me now.

He gave me a look of despair and said lamely, "She wished, too."

"Oh no!" I said. "Where have they gone? What did they wish for?"

But, of course, I could guess.

"They've gone to the *Argot*. They've gone to help," Wilfred said.

"But how?" I asked. "They don't know anything about planes, do they?"

"Zebediah's gone to join Father, and Winifred has gone to try to rescue them both. Zebediah will just egg Father on. He wants to be a pilot, too. He doesn't understand what has happened. Neither Father nor Zebediah has any *sense*. And Winifred will never convince them of the seriousness of the situation. I have to go. I can explain to Father what has happened and that he must turn the plane around before the three of them are shot down."

And saying so, Wilfred scrambled up and over the fence just as Sina caught sight of us and came racing out of the house. She joined me just as Wilfred disappeared.

"Then it is true," she whispered, her hand an icy grip on my arm. "Always I have wondered but never been sure."

She continued to stare at the place where a minute ago Wilfred had stood.

"Oh, Sina," I said. "What are we going to do? The three of them have gone to join their father. If the plane is shot down, they're all going to be killed."

At that moment we saw Old Tom coming out of the woods on his way back from the hermit's and we ran to tell him what had happened.

"They've gone there? To the plane?" he said. "Are you sure?"

"Where else?" I asked. "Did you talk to the hermit?"

"He remembers nothing," said Old Tom, panting, as we raced back to the night garden. "That's the trouble. Things float in and out of his head. He doesn't deny telling Zebediah about the access code, but he doesn't remember it either. I could see he was going to be no help. Well, I didn't like to say so before, but this man, their father, must be mentally unhinged. No sane person would steal a plane in times of war without understanding the consequences. And those three children are at his mercy now."

"Oh, Tom, you don't really think?" said Sina.

"Of course, I think so! And now *I'm* going to have to go!" said Old Tom.

"I'll go, too!" I said.

"Don't be ridiculous, Franny. If anything happens to me, you're all Sina's got. Besides which, you'd only be underfoot!" barked Old Tom.

We had reached the night garden. Before anyone could say anything else, Old Tom climbed up and over the fence and the last thing he yelled, in tones of supreme irritation, before disappearing was, "Never, ever, ever have houseguests!"

And then it was only me and Sina, a sky full of stars, and the night garden.

We stood staring, our mouths agape. And if you think UFOs and ghosts are sufficient preparation for taking in stride four people disappearing into thin air before your very eyes, then you have not had enough experience with the world of the unseen.

"Now what?" said Sina over and over. "*Now* what?"

But I, for one, was fresh out of bright ideas.

+ ✦ +

At the same time we stood there gaping, Old Tom suddenly found himself with his own jaw hanging as he stared around the inside of a loud airplane. It was Old Tom's first time on an airplane, and he decided there and then it would be his last. Initially he was only conscious of the great rattling roaring noise, the shaking of the plane, and a peculiar smell. But once he was slightly oriented and had a chance to look about his heart dropped, for there in the cockpit lay a man he could only guess was Fixing Bob, slumped over the plane's instruments and on the floor, lying as neatly side by side as if they'd been placed there, were Winifred, Wilfred, and Zebediah. All unmoving. All dead.

At first Old Tom could only stare. He was confused and dizzy and the funny-smelling air seemed to be making him sick. He just gazed down at the bodies of the children and thought how they had followed their father one by one into uncertainty and death. What an extraordinary thing love and families were. How the children would rather follow their father into folly, doomed to prison or death, than let him or each other go it alone. How unhappiness in one person in a family is taken on by everyone else. That they would rather join the unhappy party in his unhappiness than isolate him by leaving him to it. And now there were four-fifths of this family, lying dead. Crying Alice would really never recover from this. No doubt she would do herself in rather than survive it. If you want to do something for your family, old Tom thought, be happy. Let them join you *there*. He knew he should be doing something, trying to figure out the plane controls. Or the radio to signal distress. *Something.* But all he could do was stare down at those three little bodies and cry.

THE GROUND

ina and I continued to stand there saying nothing, but our brains were each working furiously.

Finally Sina said, "I can't think of anything to do but to go see the hermit again. He may not remember telling Zebediah the access code, but perhaps he will remember some way to bring the plane back."

"I have an unused wish," I said. "Why don't I just wish them all back here safe and sound?"

"You can't," said Sina. "You remember the story of Maria May: you can't *un*wish something. And we tried once with something I wished. I wasn't sure . . . I hadn't been sure my wish had worked."

"What?" I asked. "What did you wish?"

"We haven't got time to go into that now. Now we

must find out what the hermit knows about this plane and see if he can think of a way to help them."

"How?" I asked.

"I don't know," she said. "But one thing I've learned, Franny, is that not only do I not know everything, but there's lots of things people know that I don't even know that I don't know. When you've got a problem, find an expert, and don't assume they won't find a solution just because you can't imagine any way to fix the problem."

So I ran to get flashlights and we made the long trek in the dark, looking up periodically hoping to see the *Argot*, but we could neither see nor hear anything that sounded like a plane.

✦ ✦ ✦

When we got to the cabin the hermit didn't answer our knocks. We tried to open the door, but he had a latch on the inside so Sina had to break the door in.

"Oh dear, I feel so rude," she said.

The hermit was asleep in a corner of his cabin. Sina charged up to him, shined her flashlight in his eyes, and said, "Wake up! For God's sake, wake up!"

But the hermit continued to snore, so she reached down and shook his shoulder.

"You must wake up. It's an emergency," she said.

At this word the hermit not only popped awake but was on his feet in seconds, making incoherent noises that must have been sleep talk and pulling on his pants.

"Please, you have to help us," pleaded Sina. "You must tell us everything you know about the *Argot*. It's been stolen and we must get it back."

The hermit just stood staring at us. His body had reacted from long practice to an emergency situation, but his mind couldn't take it in.

"Oh, Sina, this is no good," I wailed. "He doesn't even understand us."

"Don't you remember," Sina pressed on, "how Old Tom came to ask you about the *Argot*? Because the children's father, Mr. Madden—Fixing Bob, as he calls himself—has taken it. Because of the code you helped send him. If you knew the code, you must know something about the *Argot*. You must be able to help us get it back."

The hermit still stood in mute incomprehension.

"The *Argot*. The *Argot*!" repeated Sina, as if trying to jam the word into his brain and shake something loose.

But as he stood looking confused, Sina began to cry. Whether this was in frustration or grief I could not tell. I had never seen Sina cry before. It shook me as much as any of the events of that night.

"There are three children who will die. And Old Tom, who went to rescue them. Please. Please," Sina pleaded. "They'll be shot down. You must have known something when you gave Zebediah the code. Now he's gone to join his father. Zebediah made a wish in the night garden."

"Zebediah?" said the hermit, and something awoke in him. You could see it in his eyes: a light behind all the misted confusion of his poor, injured brain. "Zebediah? *Where* is Zebediah?"

"Well, we don't know for sure, but we think he wished himself to be with his father on the *Argot*."

"He can't be on the *Argot*," snapped the hermit. "They haven't worked out all the bugs yet."

"But he is," I chimed in. "Zebediah's father, Mr. Madden, has *stolen* it. The air force is out to shoot it down as soon as they see it. They think it's full of Japanese spies. And then Zebediah . . . Zebediah will be killed."

"The air force is probably less concerned than they are giving out. It may go for a time, but it won't go indefinitely. It's unlikely it will fly for the kind of periods of time the air force has claimed. It's a tool for saber rattling," said the hermit, roughly impatient. He no longer looked dull and confused. You could see the kind of man he had been before the cold waters got him.

"But Fixing Bob and everyone on the radio, the air force itself, is calling it a long-distance surveillance plane. They said it can fly for days without refueling," said Sina.

"Yes, yes," barked the hermit. "That's the story given out. That's the official story, but the truth is quite different."

"But Fixing Bob must have known what it's really capable of. He's maintained it for years," I argued.

"Oh, maintenance!" scoffed the hermit. "Why would anyone entrust such a secret to maintenance? I'm telling you, it's only a matter of time. That plane is going down."

"It's already been up for hours," I said.

"Where would they have taken it for that period of time?" asked the hermit. "More than likely they've already crashed somewhere remote and just haven't been found."

"Oh no, oh no," cried Sina, leaping around and biting her knuckles.

"And if they haven't, they will soon," said the hermit.

"Zebediah and Fixing Bob don't know that!" I cried. "So they're going to keep flying until they explode!"

"It won't explode," said the hermit. "It will just lose altitude and crash."

"Oh no! Oh no!" cried Sina.

"Then Zebediah will *crash*." I thought it best to keep putting Zebediah's name before him, as this seemed to tether the hermit's brain to some kind of here and now. "Zebediah will die! Zebediah will die!"

"But you must have known Fixing Bob was going to try to fly that plane," Sina said, "because Zebediah said you gave him the access code to give to his father. You helped him print it!"

"I gave Zebediah the access code because he wanted to know how the plane started," said the hermit. "He never said his father wanted to take it up."

"Well, what did you think he wanted it for?" I wailed.

"I don't know," said the hermit, rubbing his forehead in frustration. "I don't know!"

"Never mind that," said Sina. "I'm sure you meant no harm. But now they *are* in harm's way. They are very much in harm's way. They're going to crash somewhere over the ocean and die."

"No! I won't let that happen," said the hermit quietly. "I must do something. I *will* do something."

"Yes, but what? That's why we came. What can be done? Think!" I cried.

I expected I don't know what. I guess I expected him to think of some code to bring the plane back, but even then, how would we get the code to them?

"I can go," I said. "I have a wish. I could bring them the news that they must land before the plane loses altitude and crashes."

"No, Franny," said Sina, wringing her hands.

I turned to the hermit to see if he had thought of a way to help, but instead of saying something he shot out of the cabin like lightning. He didn't even have a flashlight but went tearing along the coastal trail by moon and starlight, as if all the world were to him now a night garden, lit and luminous with the life that exists without all our trying. As Sina and I tore down the trail after him, it was as if everything was illuminated with something our earth was reflecting back from the larger universe beyond. For a moment it was as if I knew something. And then as it always is when you think you have grasped it, it is gone, ungraspable, mysterious, untenable, a glimmer disappearing into the far larger night. I was running, trying to work this out as if it mattered. But really all that mattered to me at that moment was that Old Tom—*Old Tom*—was on that plane. I chased after the hermit. Sina far behind us tried to keep up, although finally she fell out of sight. Sina was never much of a runner.

"Wait!" I called as the hermit reached the fields and made for the night garden. "You need me. I can wish."

"*I'm* going. I have an unused wish, too," he called over his shoulder as I tore across the field after him. "I'm going to fly the plane back. I know how to fly it, and I know how to land it safely. Don't come. There's no point—you'll just be in the way."

Then he charged forward at twice the speed, and from afar I saw him vault over the fence into the night garden and disappear.

✦ ✦ ✦

When the hermit wished himself onto the *Argot*, he found himself standing next to Old Tom, who was stupefied and dizzy, gazing at the children, tears streaming down his face.

"They're dead," he said, grabbing the hermit's arm,

but he hardly seemed to be registering the hermit's sudden appearance.

The hermit squatted down, put his fingers to each child's neck, and said, "No, they're not. They've been gassed, but they're still alive. Their father must have pushed the gas button accidentally. You'll be down beside them in a second if we're not fast."

"Whah?" said Old Tom, swaying.

The hermit wasted no more words. He got a gas mask on himself and put one on Old Tom. Then he showed Old Tom how to get the children oxygen from a tank and get masks on them as well. After that he went to the cockpit.

"Why didn't *I* check to see if they were alive? Why didn't I try to resuscitate them? Old fool!" said Old Tom.

"You were gassed and didn't know it. You couldn't think straight but never mind that now—come help with this man," said the hermit.

"Is he alive? Mr. Madden?" asked Old Tom.

"Yes, alive and probably in better shape than the children. He's bigger, you see. Here, finish with the children and get some oxygen into him and a gas mask on him as well. I'm going to get the plane turned around.

Right now we're heading west across the ocean. When we get back over Vancouver Island you all are going to depart the plane and I'm going back out to sea where I won't be detected, to circle the island if it will stay up that long until first light, when I can see to land it on the water."

Everyone was waking up. The oxygen had revived them, and the gas masks kept them from breathing in any more sleeping gas. They were moved into seats where they slumped dizzily, barely able to take in what was happening.

"Am I having my teeth done?" asked Winifred confusedly, because it reminded her of the time she had been given gas at the dentist's.

"We're all having our teeth done. Whee!" said Fixing Bob, who had woken up and, unlike everyone else, seemed to have been made lively by the gas. He got out of his seat and tried to sit on the hermit's lap. The hermit shoved him roughly aside.

"You pushed the wrong button," said the hermit. "You don't know anything about this plane, do you? Not what any of the buttons do. Not how to fly it. Certainly not about how it may self-destruct."

"I flew the plane! I flew the *Argot*, the greatest flying

fortress in the world! I'm not Fixing Bob anymore. I'm Flying Bob! From now on you, everyone, must call me Flying Bob!"

"You're an idiot," said the hermit. "You pressed the gas button and almost got yourself and your children killed."

"Did not," said Fixing Bob contentiously. "And who the heck are you?"

"I don't know," said the hermit. "Not the point. Now keep out of this chair and let me fly."

"Oh, I see," said Fixing Bob. "My poor oxygen-starved brain has made you appear to fly us to safety. Good job, brain!" He stood up and leaned dizzily over the hermit.

"Get out of here," said the hermit rudely, shoving him aside again. "Have you had this plane in the air the whole time since you stole it?"

"Well, I'm not sure," said Fixing Bob. "I may have landed it a few times for fun. All right, maybe I *did* forget the code and had to stay grounded until I remembered. But I *did* remember. I'm a genius! Whee! And I didn't steal it—I borrowed it. And furthermore . . . who's asking?"

Fixing Bob seemed to think this was hilarious and fell

over laughing next to Winifred, who said tersely, "Don't get too close; I think I'm going to throw up."

"Don't throw up in your gas mask!" said Fixing Bob gaily. "That would make a great song lyric. Wouldn't that make a great song lyric?" And he started to sing loudly.

The hermit got the plane under control and headed back to Vancouver Island. Then he turned around in his seat and surveyed the others.

"Right," he said. "Zebediah, stop looking so scared. I'm going to fly the plane to the farm. I want the five of you ready to parachute. There are parachutes in the overhead. Fixing Bob—"

"*Flying* Bob," corrected their father.

"Flying Bob knows where."

"Right. I certainly do. I know where everything is on this plane. Just ask me. Ask me where something is. Anything. Anything."

But they all stared at him in disbelief that he could be so obtuse about their situation.

"Anyhow," Flying Bob went on when it was clear there were no takers, "clearly my brain has put this idea in the mouth of the pilot I have hallucinated. What a fine brain I have. Good job, brain."

"I don't know how to parachute! And something's wrong with Daddy," cried Winifred. "I'm scared."

"Your father is fine. He just thinks we're all imaginary," said Old Tom. "He doesn't know how you got here because he doesn't know about the night garden."

"That's right," said Flying Bob and then started another chorus of "Don't throw up in your gas mask."

"Don't worry about parachuting," said the hermit. "Easiest thing in the world. I could teach a chipmunk to parachute. And you won't be alone. I'm going to put the *Argot* on automatic pilot, and *you*"—he pointed to Old Tom—"will be jumping with this boy." He pointed to Wilfred. "And *you*, you idiot"—he pointed to Flying Bob—"will be jumping with this girl and Zebediah. We're going to harness you together. Nobody will be jumping alone. The grown-ups will pull the cord—I'll explain how—and all you children have to do is float through the air."

"Heck, I know how," said Flying Bob. "I've studied parachuting. I love everything about planes."

"Well, that's a help," said the hermit. "You're going to have to keep an eye out and stay close to this guy, then." He pointed to Old Tom. "If he forgets to pull his cord, I'm counting on you to remind him. Yell, 'Pull the cord,' and keep yelling it until he does. I'm going to show both of you"—he nodded to Wilfred—"how to work it. Let this one"—he nodded at Old Tom—"try it first, but if he fails, you do it."

Wilfred nodded.

Everyone stood quietly while Flying Bob got two parachutes out. Then the hermit gave them a short tutorial on parachuting.

Flying Bob interrupted at intervals saying, "That's right. Obviously my hallucinating brain is remembering all of this to put in the mouth of my hallucinated pilot friend to tell me. The brain. What a machine! Especially mine! Whee!"

The others ignored him. If you are about to jump out of an airplane in the dark, you are pretty much focused on that.

"I'm glad it's nighttime," said Winifred when the hermit opened the door to the plane. "I couldn't do this if I could see the ground."

"I see something ahead," said Zebediah, looking down. "Look, it's glowing."

"That's the night garden," said the hermit. "When it's directly below, you jump."

"Oh no, oh no, oh no," said Winifred.

"What about you?" Zebediah asked the hermit. "Where's your parachute?"

"I don't need one. I'm circling the plane and landing on the water at first light. I'm aiming to land close to my cabin."

"Why don't you let the plane crash and jump with us?" asked Zebediah.

"It might crash on someone's house," said the hermit. "We're going to make sure there are no casualties tonight. Not like last time."

"What last time?" asked Zebediah.

"I don't know," said the hermit, looking confused and worried for a moment.

"You can't land a plane on the water," said Zebediah.

"Yes you can. I've done it many times," said the hermit. "And if I get close enough I can swim to shore."

Old Tom looked at him disbelievingly. "The waters are freezing. Land on one of our fields, man, I beg you."

"We need to get rid of the evidence," said the hermit. "Unless you want the children's father going to prison. And maybe the children. Maybe Zebediah. The plane will sink and leave no evidence that any of us were on it."

"You can't swim to your cabin. The waters there are full of rips," said Old Tom.

"Don't worry," said the hermit. "The mermaid will save me. She did it once before. Here we are. Jump, you have to jump *now!*" And grabbing hold of Flying Bob's arm, he pulled him to the door.

With a *"Wheeeeee!"* Flying Bob and Zebediah and Winifred went soaring into the night. Then Old Tom and Wilfred stepped to the edge of the door. And before they could look down they were out into the chill air, falling above the earth and below the moon.

"Pull the cord!" screamed Wilfred.

"Pull the cord! *Wheee!*" screamed Flying Bob.

And that's when Old Tom became Very Old Tom because, he said, he aged another hundred years on that night, on that jump, in that first moment of having nothing about him but the chill night air. He panicked for a moment as he flew toward the earth, and then he remembered Wilfred tied to him and a cold calm came over him and he pulled the cord. At first it was as he feared when he thought it wouldn't work: it was going to be a free fall into nothing. But then above him the parachute inflated and down they floated through the night with the moonlight on the ocean and the glow of the night garden to guide them.

+ ✦ +

Sina and I were sitting on the back steps, grinding our teeth and wringing our hands, waiting, waiting for what we didn't know. At first, the sound of the plane was the merest rumble. Since we often heard rumblings from the Department of National Defense property down the coast, we didn't dare hope but then we knew suddenly for sure it was a plane, a large plane, *our* plane, and we ran into the field, looking up.

So much of experience is wasted on us at the time. What Sina and I saw might have filled our hearts with wonder had we not been so hysterically worried. We saw the bodies fly from the plane and for a sickening moment we thought they'd been thrown to their deaths. But then suddenly, like night-blooming flowers, the parachutes opened and the two figures floated for a time between the stars. Initially we thought there were only two people dangling there, but finally, as they got closer to earth, we realized that the two parachutes were bringing down bundles of bodies.

Sina and I ran to the closest one, which landed in the field.

I got there first and knelt beside them where they lay.

"Oh, are you all right? Are you all right?" I cried over and over.

"We're fine, Franny, let us get our breath," said Old Tom, who was stunned and gasping.

"I thought it was a lost cause. For the last hour I thought all of you who had left were a lost cause," I said somewhat incoherently.

"Well, we're not," said Old Tom, still trying to collect himself and somewhat incoherent himself.

"Where are the others?" asked Wilfred, starting to sit up.

And then we saw it through the woods. Flashlights.

"Oh my God," I said. "The soldiers."

After that things swung into action very fast.

Before I knew it, Old Tom was on his feet. "Quickly, Franny, you and Wilfred grab the parachute, take it back, and hide it somewhere. I'm going to help Sina."

Sina, having ascertained that Old Tom and Wilfred were all right, had already run toward the parachute that had landed on the beach. Wilfred and I gathered the parachute and went racing back to the house. It would all be for naught if the soldiers caught us. Old Tom ran to the beach to help out there.

"Help!" Winifred was crying. "Someone help."

Later Winifred said that she wished she hadn't been so completely positive she was going to die because she might have enjoyed the ride down more. The night garden particularly was bathed in heavenly light, and the ocean sparkled with the moon. It would have been beautiful, for a moment it almost was, despite everything, once it was clear everyone had remembered to pull the cord correctly and the parachutes had inflated as they should and there was a pleasant, slow drift toward the fields. But then a minute later a sudden gust of wind took their parachute and for a sickening moment she thought they were going to be blown out to sea. Before that happened, though, the parachute caught on the rocky cliff by the cove. Flying Bob grabbed Zebediah and Winifred because it was clear that the three of them were going to smash into the rocky cliff edge. He pulled them in tighter and held them against his body, hoping to shield them from the rocks. A second later Winifred felt with a sickening thud her father's body hit the boulder, and she and Zebediah rolled off him as best they could. Winifred was immediately alarmed because their father did nothing to help disentangle them but lay ominously still.

"Daddy!" screamed Winifred as she tried to pull herself and Zebediah free, but he did not answer.

"What's the matter with him?" asked Zebediah.

Winifred only gasped. She was looking down at the rock beneath her father's head to the gathering dark pool of blood.

The Long Night

ina flew across the field and squatted beside Winifred and Zebediah.

"Hush," she said. "Hush. There are soldiers coming."

Old Tom reached them a second later. He wasted no time but whipped his Swiss army knife out of his pocket and cut the children and Flying Bob free.

"They must have seen the parachutes," he said, pointing to the lights like fireflies in the distant woods.

"They heard the plane," said Sina.

"All right, quickly, Winifred, quickly, Zebediah, gather the parachute and take it back to the house. Wilfred and Franny are looking for a place to dispose of them."

"I know where," Zebediah piped up.

"Well, go tell Wilfred and Franny," said Old Tom. "And then go to bed. We must all look as if we've been sound asleep."

"But Daddy's hurt," said Winifred.

"Yes, he's hit his head," said Sina, gently examining the gash on the back of it. "He's certainly had a concussion. How much more serious, it's impossible to say. Old Tom and I will deal with it."

Old Tom nodded as he whipped off his shirt, and Sina tied it around Flying Bob's head.

"I can assess things when we get him inside," Sina continued. "If it's too serious and we must get a doctor, then we shall simply have to reveal the truth or think of a brilliant lie to explain it. I did nursing during the last war and saw a lot of head injuries, but I'm not a doctor. I *think* it doesn't look too bad. If he recovers consciousness and we wake him periodically to check on him during the night, we may be okay to keep him with us and out of the hospital. But nobody must know we have him until we have a plan. For now, hurry, get rid of the parachutes and get to bed. Quickly!"

There was no need to say more. Old Tom got covered in blood despite the shirt wrapped around Flying Bob's head. But he and Sina managed to get Flying Bob back to the house before the soldiers came. They got him into one of the maid's rooms, where Sina bandaged him. Old Tom cleaned up the blood and dirt that was on the floor downstairs and then hightailed it upstairs to change into his pajamas.

"Turn off all the flashlights!" he hissed as we heard footsteps outside. "Now! And don't make a sound!" Then he croaked frantically, "Franny! The parachutes!"

"Gone," I whispered from my room.

I had no time to say more, for at that second there was a knock on the door.

Old Tom went slowly down to answer it, trying to appear as if he had just woken up. There before him was a soldier.

"I'm sorry to disturb you, sir," said the soldier. "We thought we saw lights here at the house."

"You may have," said Old Tom. "We heard a plane, you see."

"Yes, sir," said the soldier. "That's why I'm here. Our soldier manning the gun at the point thought he saw parachutists. They couldn't have been ours; we would have been told about it in advance had there been drills on of some kind."

"Perhaps one of our planes went down," said Old

Tom. "And the men had to parachute to safety. Or perhaps it was the Americans."

"Perhaps. But in that case they would come to the first house they saw, yours, thinking you might have a telephone. Or, if they knew where they were, they would come to the barracks," said the soldier.

"Perhaps they already have," said Old Tom. "If I were you, I would go back to the barracks to check."

"Yes, sir, we will certainly check, and we have left a man there in case. In the meantime, don't tell your wife, sir. It's sure to frighten her. Or the children. Or Gladys. We think the plane may well have crashed after the enemy soldiers parachuted."

"You know Gladys?" said Old Tom, changing the subject.

"Everyone knows Gladys," said the soldier and then blushed. "She's a heck of a poker player and, a, um, swell cook."

"Have you actually eaten anything she's cooked?" asked Old Tom in amazement but the soldier insisted on sticking to the point.

"The thing is, sir, we're thinking it might have been spies."

"What kind of spies?" asked Old Tom.

"Enemy spies," said the soldier. "Japanese, perhaps. You've heard about the plane that disappeared up island? The *Argot*?"

"You can't think this has anything to do with that?" asked Old Tom, all agog.

"We don't know, sir. We'll keep a soldier here to guard you, but if it's Japanese spies, it's doubtful they'd head here. More likely they've made for the woods, where they'll hide until daylight. But don't worry. The entire barracks is out scouring the coast for them."

"You don't think, perhaps, the gunner was mistaken? I mean, he might have fallen asleep and dreamt it. All alone, just watching the night sky hour after hour, these guards must drift off all the time. I can't blame them. I'd sleep away my shift myself," suggested Old Tom hopefully.

"Sir, my men don't sleep. They're made of sterner stuff."

"How stern?" said Old Tom. "Define 'stern.'"

But the officer could not be drawn into any kind of philosophical nit-picking. "And several of the men in the barracks also heard a plane."

"Might they not all have been dreaming?" suggested Old Tom. He knew this sounded lame. He was doing the best he could, suffering as he was from the aftereffects of being gassed and all the other excitements of the night.

"No one wants to think there are enemy spies about, but it does no good to hide from it, sir. In times of war, we must face the truth!"

"Mustn't we also face it in times of peace?" asked Old Tom, happy to discuss minute philosophical points, but again the soldier was having none of it.

"Don't you worry, sir. My men are here to protect these shores, and protect them we will!" said the soldier.

"Well, gosh," said Old Tom. "Thanks. You wouldn't consider planting some potatoes while you're at it?"

"Ha, ha, sir, good one," said the soldier. "We must keep our sense of humor in times of war!"

"Good night," said Old Tom, who had been perfectly serious. It had always seemed to him a terrific waste of manpower to have a whole barracks full of men, doing essentially nothing, when there was farmwork to be done. He closed the door and crept back upstairs, making his way to the third-floor maid's room where we had stowed Flying Bob. When he came in, Sina put a finger to her lips. I had crept up to join Sina when I heard the downstairs door close. Old Tom joined us by the side of Flying Bob's bed.

"He woke up twice," Sina said, gesturing to Flying Bob. "He's had a bad concussion, I think, and I hope nothing more. But, Tom, he remembers nothing. He doesn't know where he is or how he got here. He's never met me, so that probably further confused him."

"That's a blessing," said Old Tom. "Because he was half off his head in the plane. I wouldn't trust him not to give the whole show away if he remembered it."

"He's sleeping now. I'll keep an eye on him. I'm thinking if we can keep him away from his children and you, which might jog his memory about the events of the night, and if we can somehow put him on the roadside somewhere, maybe we can convince him that he had some kind of car accident coming down island and anything he remembers was only a dream. He must never suspect that he was the one to take the *Argot* because he is certain to be grilled intensely when he gets back to the base and he must believe his own story. But we won't know until morning just how much memory he will recover."

"It seems like a long shot," said Old Tom.

"We have to try," said Sina.

And then what followed was a very long night for me and Old Tom and Sina. Old Tom paced in the hallway

240

outside the bedroom where Flying Bob lay, while Sina and I remained at his bedside. We were hoping that he wouldn't wake up too completely but that he would wake up enough that we could be sure he hadn't slipped into a coma.

The first time his eyes fluttered open, Sina said, "What year is it, dear?"

"1945," he muttered.

"Good. Go back to sleep," she cooed.

Then half an hour later when he hadn't awoken naturally, Sina pinched him gently until he did and asked, "Who is prime minister?"

"William Lyon Mackenzie King," said Flying Bob.

This was repeated several times over a couple of hours.

Sina must have been very tired, because the fourth time this question was asked and answered her mind strayed and she asked, "Don't you really think he would look better with a mustache?"

"Whah?" said Flying Bob.

"Like Mussolini and Hitler," Sina said, and began to get worked up as she always did when she got on this subject. "Don't you think we'd be better off with a, well, a *fiercer*-looking prime minister?"

"Huh?" Flying Bob said, staring at her in disbelief. "Are you some kind of angel?"

"I'm an ordinary Canadian citizen," said Sina. "Questioning my leader's grooming choices. I mean, would it hurt him to grow his facial hair just a little? Because it's really a kind of male attribute signaling that the male in question has the proper amount of testosterone, and how can we know that if he insists on going around baby-faced? It's embarrassing, and I mean not just on a national but on an international level. On the international circuit! I wouldn't be surprised if those Italians don't go around laughing at our soldiers and calling them those sissy Canadians with their hairless leader!"

"Sina," hissed Old Tom from the hallway. "Hush!"

"Yes," I whispered. *"Xnay on the iatribeday."*

"Well, I'm just saying," said Sina, folding her arms in front of her chest and lapsing into silence.

Flying Bob gave her one last confused stare before drifting back into unconsciousness, but for many years afterward he talked about the angel who thought the prime minister should try to look a little more like Hitler.

People just thought he was mad.

All night Old Tom and Sina and I stayed awake. Even if we didn't have Flying Bob to attend to, I doubted any of us could have slept. Ironically, the Maddens, who had instigated all this commotion, slept like babies. Although, to be fair, that was probably the aftereffects of the gas.

Finally, just faintly, in early morning, the darkness began to lift. It was that filtering light before the sun rises in a rosy blast over the horizon and sends a path of sparkles across the sea.

"Come on," said Old Tom, beckoning to me from the doorway as Flying Bob snored. "Let's see if we can get to the hermit's cabin without the soldiers seeing us. The hermit said he would try to land on the water there at first light."

"Oh, Tom, you can't take Franny," said Sina.

"Why not?" asked Old Tom. "The soldiers don't suspect *us*. Nothing more natural than a man walking with his daughter, that is, if they see us at all. I know something about giving people the slip."

"What if something happens *here*?" asked Sina nervously.

"Don't lose heart now, woman," said Old Tom.

We went down the back stairs and out the door as

swiftly and quietly as mercury through a thermometer. There was a soldier in front of the house, so we made our way noiselessly for the bushes that bordered the cliff down to the ocean. From there, although the walking was a bit scratchy, we were hidden until we got to the woods.

We walked for a long time soundlessly with the brilliant light of morning creeping over the ocean. Sun sparkled on wave tips, seals splashed, ravens cawed, and sandpipers chirped. They were all the happy normal sounds of the world waking up, but the sound we most wanted to hear was the roar of the *Argot* coming to land by the cabin. Had the plane already crashed? Had the hermit died alone and unheralded at sea? We were also listening for the sound of soldiers on patrol because we would no longer be alerted by flashlights. We were so tense that although I knew it was best not to speak, I could not help myself. I groped for any topic but the fate of the hermit.

"If we only had a dog," I said finally. "A dog would alert us to men in the bushes."

"A dog would alert the men in the bushes to us," countered Old Tom.

"Still, when this is over, let's get a dog."

"Good idea, Franny," said Old Tom. "Let's."

"What kind?" I asked.

"I've always wanted a collie," said Old Tom.

"What, you mean like Lassie?"

"Yes."

"Okay, let's get a collie. Why haven't we gotten one before?"

"I don't know," said Old Tom. "There's all kinds of things you mean to do but don't get around to."

"Who is going to put Flying Bob on the side of the road? And where?" I asked.

"Yes, I've been wondering that, too," said Old Tom. "And I'm thinking that, rather than leaving him on the side of the road, we need someone to be in the accident *with* him. We need someone to drop him there unconscious and when he has a moment of consciousness as he has had off and on all night, to tell him how he got there. She needs to say that he was hitchhiking and then there was a car accident and he hit his head. In other words, *she* must remember being in the accident. And it must look as though there *was* an accident. Which means we must use a car that can get dinged. And not our truck—that would be too suspicious."

"Who would be willing to do that?" I asked. "Who

would have a car that they'd be willing to smash up and can also keep a secret because she will have to be in on it?"

"I've been thinking all night about it," said Old Tom. "And I believe I have the answer. Miss Macy!"

And then we both jumped a foot in the air because just as he said Miss Macy, she appeared, suddenly bursting through the bushes like a vision in khaki.

"OH!" she cried. "I thought you were a bear!"

"Shhh!" said Old Tom. "The place is crawling with soldiers."

"Well, why shouldn't it be?" asked Miss Macy in her usual loud and cheerful tones.

But before we could answer, we heard it. We *heard* it, the sound of a plane engine overhead. I was almost afraid to look up for fear that it would be some other plane, maybe sent to scout for the enemy spies, but Old Tom grabbed me, pointing upward at the plane making its way down to land on the water, and began to run.

"Oh no!" I cried, because I saw from far away down the coast the sentinel who stood posted atop the cliff point start to run, too. "The sentinel has spotted it!"

"Come on, Franny! *Hurry*, we must get to him before the soldiers do!"

GLADYS STEALS A CAR

ld Tom, Miss Macy, and I ran like furies. By the time we reached the cabin, the plane was down, floating on the water. The hermit had landed it in the cove, close enough in that no one who wasn't between the two points of land forming it could see it sinking, but far enough out that it would sink completely underwater. It was a brilliant place to put it, and we could only hope that there were no soldiers in the cove when it went down. The beauty of its landing, which we missed, would have been wasted on us probably, because, as I have said, so much of experience *is* wasted because our emotions are all in the way.

As we got there, it was going down fast. We saw the hermit, perched on the wing; then he dove and we saw nothing for the longest time except the plane going under, creating a swirl of water around it. The ocean wasn't unusually rough, but there are always waves and we could see rips, so we watched frantically for the hermit's head to appear. When it did, I grabbed Old Tom.

"He's too far out!" I said frantically. "He's being pulled by a rip."

"Give him a chance," said Old Tom tensely. "See if he can swim across it."

We watched, biting our lips, as the hermit made his way across the rip, swimming as he ought, not fighting it, but we could see he was making no headway.

"He'll be pulled out to sea. He'll drown!" I said.

"I'll go after him," said Old Tom, taking off his shoes.

"You'll drown, too!" I said. "You know you can't swim well enough."

Old Tom, for all his years by the ocean, hated the water, didn't swim well, and never got into it if he could help it.

"I've got to try," said Old Tom.

"Oh dear," I said, because I knew there was no dissuading him then.

"Well, honestly, am I going to have to do this every two years or what? This is getting to be monotonous," said Miss Macy in exasperation.

She further amazed us by stripping down to her underwear in two seconds flat. But what was even more amazing was that underneath her khaki uniform she wore gold-sequined underpants and bra.

"A Girl Guide never wavers!" she shouted, and plunged into the sea, greatly exciting the cormorants and gulls that thought they had that patch of sea to themselves.

Miss Macy swam out toward the hermit in swift, measured strokes as if she did this every day. She then quite competently wrapped her arm around the hermit's chest and swam back to shore. While she did this, I ran into the woods to the hermit's cabin and grabbed a blanket and a towel. I gathered up Miss Macy's clothes and, once she and the hermit had reached the shore, threw the blanket on the hermit and the towel to Miss Macy and we hustled them immediately into the woods.

"It will take the sentinel a while to get here, but other soldiers are sure to have seen the plane, if not landing, at least heading this way," said Old Tom as we ran deeper into the forest. "We must get the hermit out of here. I don't know how we'll get him to our house without being seen. And seen *wet*."

"We'll bushwhack to my place," said Miss Macy. "I'll hide him there."

"But you don't even know what this is about," I said.

"A Girl Guide is a friend in need, that's all I need to know," said Miss Macy.

I was suddenly glad as could be that she was a bit touched. A sane person would have certainly had questions or reservations at this point.

The hermit wasn't looking any too sprightly. He kept staring at Miss Macy and saying, "You did come. I knew you would."

"Well, I'll thank you to stop landing in the water like that," said Miss Macy acidly. "It's getting to be a *bore*. It's not like I enjoy morning swims in my skivvies. As you can see, salt water is simply heck on sequins. They're falling off all over the place. I'll never recover half of them. Do you have any idea how much sequined underwear *costs*?"

"I'll pay for them," said the hermit drowsily.

"You don't have any money!" I said, and then wished I'd bitten my tongue.

"Never mind. I'll pay for them," snapped Old Tom. "If we're all well enough to be arguing about who's paying for the underwear, we're all well enough to skedaddle a little faster before the soldiers come."

And then we split up, Miss Macy and the hermit

through the woods, and Old Tom and I back to the coastal path and our house, trying to move quickly and yet look casual in case we were spotted. Twice we saw foot patrols bursting through the woods to head toward where the plane landed. Fortunately none of them passed close enough to see us squatting for cover when we heard them, and we hoped none of them ran into Miss Macy and the hermit but had no way of knowing. It was all very wearing.

But once back at the house, it became more wearing because we had to plan what to do next. I pulled Sina into the hallway and we related everything that had occurred so far to her and the Madden children, whom she had had to kick out of Mr. Madden's bedroom earlier to keep him from seeing them and coming into the here and now. It seemed to me the whole night was about getting some people into the here and now and keeping others from it. Currently it was a matter of getting Flying Bob out of the house and up island.

"We can't use Miss Macy now," said Old Tom. "Whoever has the car accident with Flying Bob is going to have a ton of reporters and military converging on them. If Miss Macy is going to hide the hermit, we can't use her for the car accident. It's too dangerous."

"Why does anyone have to hide the hermit?" asked Winifred. "Why can't he just go back to his cabin?"

"So far, no one from the military has found or at least asked me about the cabin or the hermit," said Old Tom. "But now that the soldiers are zeroing in on where the plane landed, they might go far enough back in the woods to see the cabin, and it's too chancy if they also find the hermit. We don't know who he really is. *He* doesn't know who he really is. I always knew he had been in the air force, but I never figured him for anything very high ranking. However, it's now clear he must be someone fairly high up, because he had the code to the *Argot*. With all the attention here, someone may recognize who he is, and then they will take him away. I promised him safe refuge here. He's done what he could for his country and for all of us. We owe him that. No, we can't have people finding him in the cabin. He's safe enough with Miss Macy for now. But not if she becomes the center of attention finding Flying Bob. We need someone no one will suspect of lying. But who? Who will the military believe? Who will the soldiers trust?"

And at that moment, Gladys came tripping into the house saying, "Breakfast anyone?"

Well, it took a while. We had to explain it to her three times. She would have to take Mrs. Brookman's car, and we'd have to think of a good reason why she would have done so without telling Mrs. Brookman. Mrs. Brookman didn't have a dreadful old clunker like Miss Macy had. She kept her Nash touring car in top-notch working condition in her garage and only drove on Sundays unless there was a very pressing need. She wasn't going to be too happy with Gladys when she found out Gladys had stolen it and banged it up besides.

"And why am I doing this again?" asked Gladys, who was sitting down, eating her own burnt eggs and toast with gusto.

"Because you're saving an entire family," said Old Tom. "You must see that."

"Yeah, right," said Gladys. "I said, why am *I* doing this?"

"We don't have time for long explanations," I wailed. "You have to get going now!"

"Jeez, you're not getting it. But never mind, I'll make it easy for you," said Gladys. "I do something for you, and you do something for me."

"What?" said Old Tom. "What do we do for you?"

"I want to go to cooking school," said Gladys.

"What?" we all said. We were like a badly fed, sleep-deprived Greek chorus.

"That's right," she said, squirming a bit uncomfortably. "I . . . well, I love cooking."

"You *love* cooking?" I said.

"Since when?" asked Old Tom.

"All right, I didn't say I was the best at it," said Gladys. "But that's what cooking school is *for.*"

"I don't understand," said Old Tom. "What do you want from us?"

"I want you to pay for it. There's a school in Toronto I want to go to. It's a culinary *institute.*" She said this as if an institute were something far grander than a school. "I want to be a chef. I want to better myself."

We all looked at her in disbelief.

"What?" she squawked defensively. "I'm supposed to want to hang out here my whole life, playing poker with soldiers? I got a cousin Bettina in Toronto I can live with, but I need a hundred bucks for tuition and I need bus fare to Toronto."

"So you just want money?" asked Old Tom.

"Yeah, that's right," said Gladys.

"Well, heck, yes," said Old Tom.

"But you can't tell anyone the truth. Not about any of this, but especially not about how Flying Bob came to be in your car," I said. "You have to lie about it until the day you die. You have to swear to us on a stack of Bibles that you'll keep silent."

"Jeez, kid, no need to get so dramatic," said Gladys. "But sure, bring on a stack of Bibles."

No one moved.

"Or even one?" said Gladys.

But it turned out we didn't have one among us.

"Well, swear on a cookbook, then," said Winifred, rushing to the kitchen to get *The Settlement Cookbook*, Sina's one and only cookbook.

"Swear on a toad," said Zebediah. Zebediah had discovered toads on the farm, and between them and an outhouse, his cup ranneth over.

"You shut up!" said Winifred and Wilfred.

"Yeah, yeah," said Gladys, airily putting her hand on the cookbook. "I swear."

So then it was a matter of Old Tom filling Sina in, and we started loading milk cans and egg flats into the truck. Then Old Tom backed the truck up behind the house where we were hoping to sneak Flying Bob quietly into its bed, and that's when the trouble began, because the soldier who was keeping us safe by hanging out on our porch came around when he heard the truck and got all chatty with Old Tom. Finally, Old Tom disengaged himself and came inside.

"How are we going to get Flying Bob into the truck without that soldier seeing?" I asked Old Tom frantically.

But fortunately at that moment the soldier knocked on our front door and said, "I hate to ask you, but do you mind if I use your outhouse? I've been out here all night."

"Sure," said Old Tom.

"NO!" we children screamed.

Old Tom and the soldier looked startled.

"Don't you remember?" I said to Old Tom meaningly. "The trouble we've been having with the outhouse? The fluggermeister is out of whack."

"Oh, yes, the fluggermeister trouble. Right," said Old Tom. "Be a better idea to, uh, go in the woods."

"And not upset the fluggermeister," said Zebediah, nodding.

"You shut up!" said Winifred and Wilfred.

"Right," said the soldier. "The thing is, I'm not

supposed to leave my station. While I'm in the woods, a Japanese spy could zip right in here. Then what?"

"The woods are just a short hike from the house," said Old Tom. "I'll stay here and guard the porch."

"No, you have to go now. With me. We must get to Brookman's before *the milk goes bad*!" I said. This suddenly sounded so much like a code phrase that I was afraid the soldier would cotton on, but he seemed to be a particularly obtuse soldier.

"I know," said Zebediah. "Wilfred and I will guard the house."

"You shut up!" Winifred and Wilfred yelled automatically.

Then Wilfred said, "Actually, that's a good idea. Zebediah and I will guard the house."

"What am I, chopped liver?" asked Winifred, but nobody paid her any attention.

"I have a whistle," said Old Tom. "The children can blow it if they see any Japanese spies. How's that?"

"Well . . ." said the soldier, crossing his legs in a way to which we were most sympathetic. We had all been there. It gave us new insight into all his pacing on the porch.

"Aw, go on," said Old Tom to the soldier, giving him a

little shove, which was meant to be friendly, I think, but which knocked the soldier down the stairs and perhaps precipitated an untimely event, if you know what I mean, because the soldier, without another word, went at a knock-kneed lope for the woods.

The rest of us together carried Flying Bob down the stairs and put him in the truck, only dropping him once.

He awoke enough to say, "Where am I?"

Sina said, "In a car accident, lovely, lovely car accident, one of the best, you're enjoying it. Now go back to sleep."

And he did in such a cooperative way that we became hopeful of our plan. To tell the truth, we were all charged up, running on adrenaline and rather enjoying it.

Then Gladys and Old Tom and I leapt into the truck and sped away toward Brookman's with our fingers crossed that we could steal Mrs. Brookman's car without anyone noticing.

There were already cars, the usual morning coffee klatch, pulled up in front of Brookman's when we got there, so Old Tom drove the truck around to the back as quietly as he could and Gladys ran inside the back door to steal Mrs. Brookman's key. She crept out, a natural felon, and waved at us to show us she had it, and then she and Old Tom and I transferred Flying Bob into Mrs. Brookman's backseat, and away Gladys sped down our long country roads to the highway to find somewhere between Sooke and Comox to have the "car accident."

Old Tom and I heaved a sigh of relief, and at that moment Mrs. Brookman came out.

"I thought I heard something going on back here. Where's my car?" she asked in alarm, looking at the open garage door and empty garage.

"Oh," I said. "Old Tom, didn't Gladys say something at dinner last night about borrowing it?"

"That's right," said Old Tom. "Although I was sure she meant to ask you first."

"But she didn't," said Mrs. Brookman. "Because she knew I'd say no. That girl has driven into more ditches than you would think humanly possible. She knows very well I'd never give her my car. It's a Sunday car. That's how I keep it so nice. And is today a Sunday?" she bellowed at us in what seemed like a very accusatory way, as if she thought we had taken her car. Which, in a way, we had, but *she* didn't know that, the suspicious old witch.

"No, it's a Tuesday," I said helpfully.

"That's right," said Mrs. Brookman. "That's exactly what it is. A Tuesday. How dare she? Well, I'll have a few words to say to her when she gets back, I'll tell you that. And what did she say she wanted with it? Where did she say she was going?"

But Old Tom and I merely shrugged.

"She must be going to meet a soldier. What else would she be doing! And how, may I ask, did she get here?" demanded Mrs. Brookman.

I panicked. We hadn't thought of that, but Old Tom, inspired by Mrs. Brookman's postulation, said, "Probably got a lift *here* with a soldier. She certainly had no idea we were coming. We haven't seen her since last night, have we, Franny?"

I shook my head emphatically no.

"A lift with a soldier to go *meet* another. That girl's going to find herself in trouble if she's not careful. Well, bring the milk and eggs into the store," said Mrs. Brookman and jerking her apron in frustration, she marched back inside.

I worried any second she would become suspicious,

but she seemed content to stew about Gladys instead and we made our escape.

"Couldn't be better. Couldn't be better," cackled Old Tom as we pulled out and drove back to the farm.

But it wasn't over. Not by a long shot.

WHAT MISS MACY FORGOT

The next thing we did was drive to Miss Macy's to make sure that the hermit and Miss Macy had gotten there all right and hadn't been apprehended by soldiers or surrendered to hypothermia. Old Tom left the truck in the driveway out of view of the house in case there were soldiers there. Then we crept onto Miss Macy's porch and peeked in the window. There we saw the hermit and Miss Macy sitting at her kitchen table drinking cocoa and talking and laughing.

"Well, I'll be," said Old Tom. "Will wonders never cease. And I thought him so shy."

"Maybe something about the accident caused him to lose his shyness," I said.

Old Tom knocked on the door. Miss Macy, still

laughing, got up to answer it. "Well, hail hail, the gang's all here," she said jovially.

"Hiya," said Old Tom as we stepped in. "I see all is well."

"All's well that ends well," said Miss Macy. "Care for some cocoa?"

"No, thanks, we'd better get back. Listen," he said, turning to the hermit, "you'd better stay here until this dies down. Is that okay with you, Miss Macy?"

"Sure, sure, the more the merrier," said Miss Macy, and she was laughing in a happy, sparkly way I'd never heard before.

"It may be for days," said Old Tom.

"Okay," said Miss Macy.

"Okay," said the hermit.

"It may be for weeks," said Old Tom worriedly.

"Okay," said Miss Macy.

"Okily dokily kay," said the hermit, and that sent them into peals of laughter again. They certainly seemed to have hit it off.

They were still laughing uncontrollably when Old Tom and I went down the steps. We could still hear them when we got to the truck. We could still hear them as we drove away.

"A match made in heaven, that," said Old Tom, which got me thinking in ways I hadn't before.

"Do you think so?" I asked excitedly, because what is more thrilling than a romance? I saw myself in a lovely pink lacy dress strewing rose petals down one of the garden paths because, of course, they'd get married on our farm. "Do you think they'll marry and live together forever? Because she is lonely and I think she'd love to have someone to take care of. And he needs someone to take care of him. I mean, he can't keep living like that alone in the woods forever."

"Why not?" asked Old Tom.

"I don't know," I said. "It's not right. And they're both touched in the head. That's a point in favor of the match," I added, although really Miss Macy didn't seem so at all anymore to me. She had swum out there when the need demanded like nobody's business and managed to get the hermit through the thick bush without soldiers finding them. I don't know many people who could have done that. Of course, there was the matter of her sequined underwear. Still, that wasn't touched, maybe just a little odd, and odd people were often the most interesting. "Oh," I said, continuing to remember, "and her house was lined with books, too. Just like his cabin. They could spend long hours just reading on the porch together. Maybe he could help lead Brownies."

"Jeez, take it easy, Franny," said Old Tom. "They were just having some cocoa and a laugh."

"From little cups of cocoa do little hermits grow," I said.

Old Tom just rolled his eyes. I tried to imagine the progeny of Miss Macy and the hermit. But to be truthful, I imagined them as kind of like Martians. A Martian kind of family. Maybe these were the aliens that Gladys predicted would be talking to Sina. No, that was supposed to happen through the radio. Well, I will say in my own confused and dazed defense that I was on hour thirty-six without sleep.

"I don't see it happening," said Old Tom.

"Then I'll never get to be a flower girl!" I wailed.

Old Tom startled and looked at me but said nothing.

Then it occurred to me that I'd passed the flower-girl age anyhow. Sleep, I thought, I needed sleep.

✦ ✦ ✦

When we got back, the soldier was still standing in front of the house guarding it. Inside, Winifred, Wilfred, and Zebediah were all quite agitated, as you can imagine. Even though Flying Bob was safe for now, we were still a long way from being in the clear. So much would depend on what he could remember of the last twenty-four hours and what he would say. Sina brought the radio into the dining room, and we sat around the table listening furiously to news reports.

At three in the afternoon the broadcast we'd been waiting for finally came. A car with a Miss Gladys Brookman had been found on a deserted road one hundred kilometers from Comox. And in it was the missing maintenance man, Robert Madden. Gladys said she had picked up Mr. Madden hitchhiking the night before. On this lonely stretch of logging road the car had hit a tree and gone into a ditch, and when she had awoken she had found Mr. Madden, injured and unconscious and the car crippled beyond repair. She had waited patiently for someone to come by and had ended up spending the night in the car. Mr. Madden, who had been taken to hospital, where doctors reported his injury serious but not life-threatening, remembers nothing, not hitchhiking, not his reason for doing so, nor even Miss Brookman. His mind is a blank, he says, except for some time he spent with a Canadian angel who wished the prime minister to grow luxuriant facial hair.

"Yes," said Miss Brookman, "he kept saying 'Angel, angel' all night in his sleep."

It was a happy reunion between Mr. Madden and his wife, Alice Madden, who has been waiting frantically in Comox for news of her husband.

"I told you he could never have stolen that plane," she said, repeatedly punching the officer who brought her to the hospital until she was subdued by doctors. It is conjectured that Mr. Madden was hitchhiking down to Sooke to see his children. But he has no explanation for why he would do this when his wife was already in Comox with the family car.

"Nothing about any of this makes any sense," he said.

When told that the *Argot* had been stolen, Mr. Madden, who, as doctors report, like many head-injury victims, has been unusually emotional, cried and said that now he would "never get to fly the *Argot*."

Mrs. Madden, who also seemed to be unusually emotional after her long ordeal, when it was thought her husband was a traitor to his country, said to her husband, "Oh, shut up and eat your rice pudding." It is surmised that things had not been happy in the Madden household for some time.

"The nerve of those reporters!" interjected Winifred at this point, but we all shushed her. We didn't want to miss a thing.

The fate of the *Argot* is still a mystery, the news announcer went on, but one man at least has been exonerated. Authorities say that they are happy that the *Argot*'s disappearance was not due to defection by one of their own.

"I never thought a red-blooded Canadian would go in with those Japanese fiends," said Lieutenant Colonel McGee. "And I have, as usual, been proven right."

Although this seemed to wrap things up, fifteen minutes later there were two more news reports: In the first, a plane had been seen that morning along the southern coast of Vancouver Island. Soldiers in the area related its seeming descent by East Sooke Farm, but no one saw it land or enter the water. Divers will be sent to look once a possible point of entry has been determined. There is some speculation that this plane is the *Argot* and, if so, it is speculated that it may have crashed and its crew escaped by parachuting. Soldiers are still looking for the parachutists, but so far there is no sign of them or their parachutes.

We all heaved a sigh of relief. So far, so good.

The second news report said that Mrs. Brookman, whose car it was that was ruined by Gladys Brookman, had been reached by phone.

"I knew she'd bash it up," said Mrs. Brookman.

When told about Robert Madden, she said, "*He* was the soldier she went up to see? A married man?" Upon hearing which and asked for a comment, Mrs. Madden dumped Mr. Madden's strawberry Jell-O on his head.

"What did *I* do?" asked Mr. Madden, who still remembers nothing.

When asked whether there had been a romance between them, Miss Brookman said, "No comment." But authorities now suspect that the meeting between Mr. Madden and Miss Brookman was not accidental, as she had previously stated. Lieutenant Colonel McGee is quoted as saying, "I am glad that we have put the hitchhiking story to rest. It never really held water, I thought. As usual I am proven right."

"Lieutenant Colonel McGee seems more concerned about continuing his usual state of being proven right than anything else," I said.

"Shh," said Winifred. "Is there more?"

But the news had moved on to Nanaimo's Slug Festival training sessions, so we switched the radio off.

We all sat silently for a moment.

"No comment?" said Wilfred.

"That's terrible!" said Winifred. "What will Mother think of Daddy now? We'll never live down the unwarranted shame and degradation."

"It's not good," agreed Wilfred.

"How do you train a slug?" asked Zebediah.

"You shut up!" said Winifred and Wilfred.

"Yes, but I have to say 'No comment' was the perfect response from Gladys," said Old Tom. "Because Mrs. Brookman, unbeknownst to *her*, may just have saved the day. The story of Gladys picking up a hitchhiker was never terribly plausible. You could hear they were already questioning why Mr. Madden would be hitchhiking when his wife was in Comox with their car. But if he were meeting Gladys, well, that's something else. And we never even thought of that. And he can never deny it because he can't remember anything. Thank heavens for Gladys's reputation and Mrs. Brookman's loose tongue."

"But it's terrible for Mother," said Winifred.

"It would be more terrible if Father went to prison, I guess," said Wilfred.

"I don't think you *can* train a slug," said Zebediah.

"You shut up!" said Winifred and Wilfred.

I was beginning to feel for Zebediah. He would be about seventy, I would guess, before he was allowed to speak in that household.

"Well," said Sina, after an awkward silence, "all's well that ends well."

And that was when soldiers began appearing at the door with hysterical and disheveled Brownies.

✷

May 8

The first Brownie on our doorstep we recognized almost immediately as Ermintrude, the first trial tyke, which was fortunate, as otherwise she might have been unrecognizable. She had sticks in her hair and one whole blackberry vine trailing from her shorts. And there were gashes where she'd obviously tripped on rocks or tree roots. She looked like someone who'd lost a battle with the wilderness.

"Why, it's little Ermintrude, isn't it?" asked Sina in cooing tones, but Ermintrude refused to bite and just sobbed hysterically.

"And a plane was seen off your coast, ma'am," said a soldier to Sina, ushering more Brownies onto the porch. "These girls say they weren't on it."

"Well, of course they weren't on it!" barked Old Tom.

"As you say," said the soldier. "Remarkable coincidence, though. Have you seen anybody else strange about?"

"They're not strange; they're Brownies," Sina said coldly.

"Yes, ma'am," said the soldier. "Have you seen anything at all suspicious, I should have said?"

But of course none of us had seen or heard a thing. We led a very quiet life.

More Brownies arrived. They were just as dirty but somewhat more composed.

"Miss Macy left us!" they cried. "She left us!"

Sina and I turned to each other wildly. The day before, when Miss Macy had said she and Cheryl were making a fire ring, it hadn't occurred to us that the other Brownies would be arriving and the campout beginning. Miss Macy must have brought them all from her place through the woods to their campsite later in the day. And Old Tom and I had assumed that Miss Macy had been out for another of her reconnaissance walks when we ran into her that morning. Not for one second had it occurred to us that she had been camping in the woods with her Brownies. And forgotten or, worse, simply abandoned them in the excitement of finding the hermit.

"Where are the others?" demanded Old Tom sharply, grabbing one of the incoming Brownies by the shoulders.

"I dunno," she said, beginning to sob, too. "Everywhere."

"Winifred and Franny, take these children into the kitchen and get them a snack," said Sina.

"You mean the leftover burnt chipped beef on toast from yesterday's lunch?" asked Winifred. "Because I doubt if they'll want it."

"No, make them whatever you girls can manage, hot chocolate if you can," said Sina. "Warm foods. Pour some warm milk over Weetabix. Use your imagination. I see more soldiers on their way with more Brownies. They must be finding them all over the woods. Hurry, we must feed them and calm them down."

Winifred seemed to cotton on to the situation and led the grubby Brownies in to be fed. They perked up remarkably at seeing the Weetabix box, so they couldn't have been too traumatized. Although, perhaps they were, because I believe they were the first people in the history of the world to perk up at the sight of Weetabix.

As more Brownies came in and we got bits and pieces of the story, it was apparent that when they woke up and found Miss Macy was gone, they had panicked and run in a dozen different directions at once.

"Honestly," said Sina to the last arriving Brownie, "what a bunch of ninnies. You find out your Brownie leader is gone and you just take off for the woods in different directions?"

"Well, have we got you all now?" asked Old Tom. "That makes twelve."

"There were thirteen of us," said the last arriving Brownie.

"So one still out there," said Old Tom, when suddenly we heard bells ringing all the way from Sooke Village and fireworks and guns going off.

"What in God's name?" said Sina.

"Turn on the radio," said Old Tom.

And that's how we found out the war had ended. Or at least ended in Europe.

We were all jumping up and down and yelling, including the soldiers on our porch.

"Let's go celebrate!" yelled one soldier.

A little girl with Weetabix dripping down her chin piped up, "But we're still missing one Brownie."

"Well, twelve out of thirteen isn't bad," said the soldier hopefully.

We all gave it a moment's thought and then Sina said, "No, I really think we have to find all thirteen."

So the soldiers went out to the woods again and Old Tom whipped over to Miss Macy's. When he reminded her that she had left an entire Brownie troop stranded in the woods, she said, "Yikes!" and came back with us to defuse the situation. She was fortunate that the soldiers had found them and brought them to our place, because that was where she had told the parents to pick them up that morning. Sina had a word with Miss Macy about giving us a little heads-up next time, which was certainly a small point given the events of the week. Miss Macy had the Brownies all packed up and ready to go with a useful story about how she had left them there to see what they would do, as dictated in the demands of their survival badge requirements, and they'd all passed! Well, all except the one we hadn't found yet. But she would order the rest of them their badges immediately! Their parents, when they arrived and were told this, beamed. Everyone was prepared to be in a splendid mood, what with the end of the war and all. That is, except for the parents of the Brownie who hadn't yet been found. But an hour later she was discovered up in a tree where she said she had climbed to escape any wild animals that might be about. We decided not to tell her about the cougar that was spied sleeping on the branch above her.

Miss Macy promised her an especially large badge that she personally would stud with gold sequins, so the last Brownie was happy. Those Brownies would do anything for a badge. And most young girls will do anything for sparkly sequins. Then the soldiers all left to get roaring drunk in town, and no one seemed much interested in the *Argot* or anything else for the next twenty-four hours.

+ ✦ +

The commander came over the next day to tell Old Tom and Sina that divers would eventually be looking for a downed plane and the military would be stationed on our property for a while still, as even though we'd licked Hitler, Japan was still a nuisance.

"But it's only a matter of time, only a matter of time," said the commander. "And I'd like to thank you again for your forbearance and your war effort."

"It was nothing," said Sina.

"*De nada,*" said Old Tom.

And that was that military-wise. They removed the

guard soldier from our house, as they had decided the parachuting Japanese spies, if there had been any, were long gone and they had given up on finding them. Or if they hadn't, they weren't informing us. There were a lot of secrets during that time. Not all in the military's keeping.

Flying Bob was given a dishonorable discharge from the air force and so lost his maintenance job because, no matter why or for what reason, it was clear he had simply awarded himself a day off and walked off the base when he should have been maintaining. No one mentioned Gladys, because they wished to spare Crying Alice's feelings and also because they were a little sick of the Maddens. Crying Alice had gone back to crying at every opportunity and the possibility of having her move her family back on base now that she and Flying Bob were re-united was so awful that the military was happy just to be rid of the two of them. Flying Bob was okay with that because he was a one-plane man and now that the plane he loved was gone, he figured he might as well get a more regular job. Also because it was clear he was going to have to spend a lot of his time for, oh, say, the rest of his life apologizing to and appeasing Crying Alice.

Naturally, Winifred, Wilfred, and Zebediah, who didn't get an opinion but had one anyway, hoped to stay on in the house they had inherited in Sooke, but Crying Alice said she was done with British Columbia and all its sad memories. She could not live in a place that had been the source of so much anxiety. She didn't mention Gladys, but we all assumed that was a factor, too. When Crying Alice and Flying Bob came to pick up the children, she announced that they would be moving to Saskatchewan.

"Saskatchewan!" said Wilfred.

"What's there?" asked Winifred.

"Nothing," said Flying Bob. "I like to think of it as one long runway."

"No, you don't," said Crying Alice. "There will simply be nothingness. There will be nothing good and nothing bad, nothing to disturb my tranquillity. No planes."

No more wishes, I thought. Those had been used. No hundreds of dresses, no motorcycles, no horses, no whatever Zebediah would have wished for. No happiness of that kind. From the things they thought would bring them happiness. Perhaps no happiness at all. Perhaps Crying Alice would always cry and Flying Bob would always yearn. But there was family. If there was to be misery, they would all be together in it. When it came to the crunch, that is what they had chosen. I pondered it again, the weight and wonder of this. What we think we want is not always what we choose. But what we choose becomes our lives.

Then, because they were saying good-bye to us, Crying Alice burst into tears and sobbed all the way to their car. Which she was driving. Flying Bob wasn't allowed to drive until they were sure his head was really all better, which wouldn't be for another year. Crying Alice seemed happy about this. She said she wouldn't feel right trusting the wheel to someone who wasn't emotionally stable.

We said good-bye to Winifred, Wilfred, and Zebediah. They drove away looking pretty dismal, but really things had turned out better than could have been expected, considering.

Then Old Tom and I went to see how the hermit was doing at Miss Macy's and tell him the military seemed to have called off the coastal hunt for spies and it was safe to go back to his cabin. If he wanted to, which he *did*, disappointing me and my romantic sensibilities considerably.

We drove him back to our place, and off he plodded over the fields.

"Well, really," I said sourly to Old Tom. "I thought two kindred souls had found each other."

"Nah," said Old Tom. "He told me that she had taken to calling him Hermie for want of a name and it just drove him crazy and he couldn't remember anything, none of the stories of her life, which she poured out in his general direction like syrup over pancakes, as he put it, and that drove *her* crazy. She kept saying, 'No, not the Mildred who was my mother's sister's step-daughter, the Mildred who was my brother Barney's maid.' And such. It gave him a headache. People who live alone usually do so for a reason."

"But still," I said.

"Still nothing, Franny," said Old Tom.

✦ ✦ ✦

Later, I walked back to Miss Macy's because I wanted to know what she was doing with sequined underwear but didn't think it was something I could ask when the hermit or Old Tom was around.

"That's all I ever wear, sequined underwear," she said, leading me to her dresser and opening the top drawer. "See?"

And sure enough it was full of gold-sequined bras and underpants.

"Wow," I said. "Where do you find it?"

"Eaton's," she said. "They carry it in the underwear department, same as the plain white stuff."

"But why?" I asked. "Why do you wear it? It doesn't look very comfortable."

"My mother always said to us, 'Girls,' she said to me and my sister, 'always wear clean underwear. In case you're ever in an accident.' And it haunted me, you know, the idea of being in an accident and taken to hospital and them finding me in some cheapo old-lady underpants, so I decided then and there to get the best, most expensive underwear I could find. That'll show them, I thought. And the best, most expensive underwear came covered in gold sequins. And glad I am that I did, as I had to strip down to it twice in the last few years to rescue that annoying hermit."

I thought about this.

"So you did rescue him twice?" I said.

"That's right," she said. "I was there when his first plane went down, too. I thought it was an accident the first time, but the second time I could see he was making a habit of it."

I nodded thoughtfully.

"You know," I said. "I think he may have thought you were a mermaid."

"He's not too bright," she said. "I think he may be a bit touched in the head."

"Well, some folks are," I said.

Then I walked all the way to the hermit's because I was determined before this whole thing was over to have all my questions answered.

He was in his garden pulling weeds.

"Hello," I said, but he just looked bashfully down and kept weeding. "I won't bother you. I won't engage you in a long conversation, and I won't stay long. I just have one question."

He looked up then.

"You wished yourself on the *Argot* with Zebediah. That means that all that time in the night garden you never once made a wish. Even accidentally. How did you manage that?"

"Nothing I wanted," said the hermit, looking at me for once.

Then he went back to weeding and, as promised, I turned around and went home.

The End of This
Particular Story

hen I got in, Sina asked me where I'd been and I told her. She and Old Tom and I sat around the kitchen table for dinner. It wasn't burnt, and the old table felt like coming home after our more elaborate dining room meals.

Sina turned a face full of sympathy to me. "Are you sad to have Winifred gone?" she asked.

"Well, sort of," I said. "But you know—houseguests."

We all ate companionably but silently for a while after that, and the sun was setting over the ocean when Old Tom went to bring the horses in. But before he left he said, "Hey, why didn't you children want the soldier to use the outhouse?"

"That was Zebediah's idea for the parachutes. He put them down the hole."

"Gosh darn it. It's going to be the work of a whole morning getting them out. We can't leave them there. Houseguests!"

"Well, Wilfred saved you some time in the potato field," I pointed out.

"Wilfred," muttered Old Tom affectionately and, smiling to himself, went whistling out to catch Tag and Molly.

Sina and I sat and had a cup of tea. She got up to get the cookie jar, then put it back when she saw it was filled with nothing but the burnt cookies Gladys had made after the police returned her to our farm.

Now Gladys was gone for good. She had left the day before. I had come into Sina's studio to tell her that Gladys was all packed up and ready for Sina to drive her to the ferry.

Sina sat enthralled listening to music, her hands unmoving on the clay.

"Where's the music coming from?" I asked, looking around for the radio.

Sina nodded to a corner cabinet where a hand-cranked gramophone was perched. "Old Tom went into town and brought that home for me, as well as a few records."

"Where's the radio?" I asked.

"I gave it to Gladys. A good-bye present. I decided I didn't want the chatter, only the music," said Sina.

"Speaking of Gladys, I think she's ready to leave," I said.

"Shhh." Sina quieted me because the Divertimento had reached the Andante.

We listened to the end and then Sina lifted the needle off the record.

"Mozart, *he* did it. *He* made it visible," said Sina.

"You mean audible," I said.

"Audible, visible, tangible," said Sina.

"Why can't we?" I asked.

"I don't know," said Sina. "There's that little hiccup in time between the glimmer of sensing it and the realization of it. And in that hiccup is all the possibility. I begin to think, Franny, that it's all there in the possibility, not in the realization. If we knew for a certainty of the existence of the UFO, the ghost, the mermaid, they would no longer excite us the same way; they would join electricity, airplanes, radio waves, babies being born, all of it taken for granted because it's realized. It's that intangible indefinable thing; that's what keeps us coming back. It reminds us there's something even more wonderful that can't be realized. It's what people are always trying to touch. It's what Gladys is looking for in her bebop and in her cooking. What Miss Macy searches for on her endless long hikes. That I long for in my sculpture, you in your writing, Tom in his garden, Flying Bob on his planes."

"Hey!" shouted Gladys from the truck. "I can't sit here all day."

So Sina went out to drive Gladys to the ferry, which she would take to the mainland, where she would catch a train to a faraway city where she knew only one person, to overcome all kinds of trials and tribulations to try and perhaps never succeed in her cooking to make that thing, that *thing* tangible. How difficult it was. But off Gladys went. Maybe not even knowing why she was going or what she was trying to find. But now I knew: she was looking to do what we all were, and I wished her luck.

"Sina," I said while we finished our tea, "you never told me what you wished for. In the night garden."

"Oh," said Sina, getting up in a fidgety way. "Let's go up to the landing."

We hadn't sat on the landing together once while the Maddens were here, so I nodded.

As we climbed the stairs I said, "Did Gladys even thank you for the radio?"

"Oh, I don't care about it anymore. I figured out that aliens aren't going to be contacting me via it. Of course," said Sina sighing, "that also means I can't believe my great gift is that I don't know how beautiful I am. It was nice thinking I was beautiful. I've never thought so, you know, being so tall. And kind of large. You know."

"But, Sina," I said honestly, "you are beautiful. And see, you *don't* know it. So that much was right."

"Oh, Franny," said Sina.

We sat on the landing and I sat on her lap on the rocking chair. Because Sina is so large and I am rather small for my age, it was still comfortable. And besides, there was only one chair because we hadn't returned the second rocker to the landing yet.

"So what did you wish for?" I asked again.

"For you," said Sina. "I cannot regret it. I cannot. But, Franny, imagine, Old Tom and I could not have children. I wished for a baby. And after that a woman puts a baby in my arms and then falls dead at my feet. The people who were to adopt the baby are dead in a fire, their home burned to the ground; who knows what befell your real parents."

It gave me a chill to hear her call someone else my real parents. Old Tom and Sina were my real parents.

"I cannot regret it either," I said. "Your wish."

"Old Tom and I wanted nothing so much as to keep you, Franny, but Old Tom said we couldn't not try to unwish it, not when there was such a cost to others, their *lives*. So he tried to use his own unused wish. He went into the garden and unwished mine. But nothing happened. I was never so happy, never so happy as when you were there still in my arms after his wish. So then what to believe? Either what he had been told was true, you cannot unwish something, or the whole thing was bunk; your appearance concurrent with my wish was a coincidence. We could never be sure. I think really we didn't want to know. I think, myself, that is why Old Tom never tried to use his wish again after that. That is, until the Maddens were in such trouble. The whole legend of the night garden might have been true, or it might not. In the end we had no real proof and we didn't have to take responsibility for all that other stuff that might have happened as a result of my wish."

"But you didn't ask for all the other stuff to happen. It just happened."

"As things do," agreed Sina.

"As things do. I've tried to write it. About the UFOs and ghost and mermaid and such. All the magic. But I can't. I can't pull it through—not *that* kind of magic, I can't use them to call up what I want to convey. I can only sense it."

"No, no," said Sina. "I can't make the clay become . . . that thing. I thought maybe giving the mermaid legs, you know, because it was really Miss Macy, but that didn't help."

And then we weren't mother and daughter or adopted mother and adopted daughter or even friends. Though I sat on her lap, we were colleagues. We understood the longing and we understood the difficulty.

And then I thought I had a brilliant idea as we rocked there so full of despair. "Sina," I said. "I have an idea."

"What?" she asked as we both gazed out to sea.

"What if we just give up? We can just stop trying."

Sina laughed.

"No," I said. "I mean it. If we didn't try . . . it would all still be here. What if we gave up having it come from us, through us, what if we gave up *us*?" It was not an easy idea to explain.

"But what would we be, then?" asked Sina.

And for a second I could see by the wild look in her

eye that as muddled as I had made this, she got it. She *got* it. We were not separate from it all, writing about it, sculpting it, in that moment we felt it differently; we *were* it, and it didn't take mermaids or UFOs or ghosts to remind us of the wonder of it. Why we couldn't feel this all the time I didn't know, but in that moment we did.

And in that moment we were not just ourselves, we had given up ourselves and because we felt it not just in ourselves, we were part of everything, the wind and the rain, the moonflowers and the moon, each other and Miss Macy and the soldiers manning the guns on the shore, the submarines and their captain and all of the crew, the grandmother whale and the baby, the elephant seal with its last gasping breath pushed back to the waves, the hermit and his mermaid, the UFO, the tide and the rain and the fog and the bats and the bugs, we were the pigs and the cows and the chickens and Flying Bob and the men looking for him and Crying Alice and the ghost, and we were the ones watching the parachuted figures, we were all that the parachuted figures saw, and we were the parachuted figures drifting gently in the stars.

And I got the rocker from downstairs and put it back next to Sina's, and we rocked side by side. And I held

Sina's hand. And pretty soon Old Tom came in, got a chair, and sat next to us, which was unprecedented, and night fell and the first evening star appeared and the windows were open and the scent of the night stock wafted up to us from the night garden.

Many thanks to:

Ian Andersen
Marie Campbell
Margaret Ferguson
Lynne Missen
Ken Setterington
Charmaine Welch